This book is a work of fiction. Characters, events, names, and locations are used fictitiously. Any resemblance to actual persons, living or dead, places, or events is completely coincidental. Any resemblence to truth is quite intentional.

DEVELOPMENT OF THE CENTRAL NERVOUS SYSTEM

Effects of Alcohol and Opiates

DEVELOPMENT OF THE CENTRAL NERVOUS SYSTEM

Effects of Alcohol and Opiates

MICHAEL W. MILLER, EDITOR
Department of Psychiatry
College of Medicine
University of Iowa
Iowa City, Iowa

WILEY-LISS

A JOHN WILEY & SONS, INC., PUBLICATION
New York • Chichester • Brisbane • Toronto • Singapore

Address all Inquiries to the Publisher
Wiley-Liss, Inc., 605 Third Avenue, New York, NY 10158-0012

Printed in the United States of America.

While the authors, editor, and publisher believe that drug selection and dosage and the specifications and usage of equipment and devices, as set forth in this book, are in accord with current recommendations and practice at the time of publication, they accept no legal responsibility for any errors or omissions, and make no warranty, express or implied, with respect to material contained herein. In view of ongoing research, equipment modifications, changes in governmental regulations and the constant flow of information relating to drug therapy, drug reactions and the use of equipment and devices, the reader is urged to review and evaluate the information provided in the package insert or instructions for each drug, piece of equipment or device for, among other things, any changes in the instructions or indications of dosage or usage and for added warnings and precautions.

Recognizing the importance of preserving what has been written, it is a policy of John Wiley & Sons, Inc. to have books of enduring value published in the United States printed on acid-free paper, and we exert our best efforts to that end.

Library of Congress Cataloging-in-Publication Data

Development of the central nervous system: effects of alcohol and
opiates / editor, Michael W. Miller.
p. cm.
Includes index.
ISBN 0-471-56125-8
1. Alcohol—Physiological effect. 2. Narcotics—Physiological
effect. 3. Brain—Effect of drugs on. 4. Developmental neurology.
5. Fetal alcohol syndrome. I. Miller, Michael W.
[DNLM: 1. Alcohol, Ethyl—adverse effects. 2. Central Nervous
System—drug effects. 3. Central Nervous System—growth &
development. 4. Narcotics—adverse effects. 5. Prenatal Exposure
Delayed Effects. 6. Substance Abuse—in pregnancy. WL 300 D497]
QP801.A3D48 1991
618.3'268—dc20
DNLM/DLC
for Library of Congress 91-22912
CIP

CALLED TO FREEDOM

Stephen L. Boehrer

A STORIED REFLECTION ON LOVE

A NOVEL

Stephen L. Boehrer

WIND-BORNE PUBLICATIONS

Also by Stephen Boehrer

Unless A Grain of Wheat: 1997
Dead Men's Bones: 2000
Published by Wind-borne Publications

Cover Design by Maryellen Miskimen

Library of Congress Control Number: 2003109082

ISBN: 0-9660607-2-5

Published by: Wind-borne Publications
P.O. Box 733 Hales Corners, WI 53130

web: www.execpc.com/windborne
e-mail: boehrer@execpc.com

First Printing: August 2003 Printed in U.S.A.

TO ALL THOSE IN MINISTRY
WHO ARE FREE ENOUGH
TO MAKE THE FREEDOM OF OTHERS
THEIR PERSONAL AND PROFESSIONAL QUEST

ACKNOWLEDGEMENTS

To my wife, Rita,
for her patience, insightful critiques
and constant encouragement.

To the following for their contributions, critiques and support:

Pastor Grace Swensen of the Evangelical Lutheran Church in America (ELCA)
Janet and Paul Stevens of Pilgrim United Church of Christ (UCC), Carlsbad, CA.
Terry Ryan
Josephe Marie Flynn, SSND
Rita and James McDonald
Judy Bridges
Jack Letellier

Remember that you have been called to freedom. Not a freedom that gives free rein to the flesh, but a freedom that, out of love, places you at one another's service.

Paul to the Galatians 5:13

CHAPTER ONE

This, the final leg of my journey, begins as it will end, with a funeral.

Now that my eyes are cast mostly toward floors, stone often greets me. Fickle stone, at times warm and protective, at others, cold and forbidding. Today, here in this great basilica, this stone chills me.

My legs have been leeched almost entirely of their starch by Lou Gehrig's disease and I spend my days in this wheelchair. The disease causes me to take an inventory of myself each morning. Today my arms retain some strength and movement, and I can wheel this chair -- on level surfaces. I can stand, but not walk. I feed myself, though I have more than once spooned oatmeal at my nose. My head has some side-to-side movement, but I find it difficult to hold it aloft for long periods. I retain the use of my voice and senses, though touch has lost much of its delicacy. I am grateful for every hint of sensation now, for the wafts of incense that interrupt the stale odor of this stone, though I am grateful for that as well. My penmanship remains legible. To sum up, I am a diminished remnant of a once portly, six-foot-two-inch man, a man reduced to an anemic imitation of Rodin's *Thinker*.

My disease has left me with a single productive capacity, to think. I am one whose life is inexorably becoming one of the mind. It is either that or no life. To retain that capacity I also take daily mental inventories and exercise. I am Fred, Frederick Patrick Sweeney. I am an Archbishop who has had the good fortune of participating in exciting times. My mentor was Cardinal Alberto Della Tevere. He was elected to the papacy as Pope Francis I, and after only a short time in office he was severely wounded in a bomber's assassination attempt. Like me, he spent these past years in a wheelchair, so incapacitated that only his tongue had movement. He could hear and he could speak -- and he accomplished great things.

I exercise my memory each day. It is said that this great basilica can hold 100,000 people. I suspect it holds that full complement today. The basilica! St Peter's Basilica! Inside it is 632 feet long, nearly double the length of St. Patrick's Cathedral in New York. From side to side at the central altar it is 462 feet wide. If you include the sacristy it covers an area of 432,756 square feet -- nearly ten acres, almost one tenth the area of Vatican City itself. The height of the dome is 309 feet, and its diameter is 138 feet. My memory is now my muscle.

As I sit here, I am trying to interpret the tears that refuse my order to cease. They are a positive sign in that my tear ducts continue to function. Truthfully, though, I would gladly yank those ducts out by the roots if I could alter the cause of my tears. Across this cold marble floor I stare at, they are burying my friend, Pope Francis I.

I am able to deal with the loss of him only in small doses, even now after these several days since his death. I suspect that the official nine days of mourning, the *Novemdiales,* likewise will not provide sufficient time for me to realize the full import of his passing. Perhaps that explains my frequent mental excursions. As I sit here in this great apse, the Altar of the Chair is at my distant right. To my left at equal distance is Bernini's magnificent Baldacchino with its twisted bronze columns surrounding the main altar.

From the sounds I hear, the Masters and Mistresses of Ceremonies are placing the covers on Francis' three coffins, one inside the other, sealing each as they are closed. The first is made of cypress wood, a symbol that the pope was human, just like all humans. The second is lead. It has the name of the pope and the dates of his tenure imprinted on it. It contains the more important documents that were stamped with his seal, and the seal itself, the fisherman's ring broken after his death. The third is made of elm, a wood considered precious in ancient Rome, to signify the great stature of the person it holds.

Soon I'll hear the chunk, chunk of the windlass as it lowers him to the crypt. His body will lie there in a spectacular tomb, but not his mind. His mind lives elsewhere. It lives in others, like me.

By his generosity, I have shared his apartment in the apostolic palace for the past several years. "We need similar care," he said to me in his staccato speech. "Come live with me and together we will exercise each other's mind." In truth, he was the trainer, I the trainee.

These tears refuse to stop, even when I redirect my mind. Some inner mind, the part that controls tears, refuses to be diverted. He is dead. "Let us exercise our minds on death," he said to me, only days ago. We faced each other from our wheelchairs in his walnut-paneled library, the one room of his apartment where he had permitted a measure of luxury, and where we spent much of our days. We both faced limited days, but I had avoided any cold, direct stare at that reality. "Are you at home with your death, Federico?" he asked.

The question brought a sudden terror, a sensation for which I was not grateful. The question carried me to a place I had refused to visit. Moreover, *death* and *at home* struck me as oxymoronic. Even though I have hope and belief in an afterlife the passage there holds no warmth for me. I can picture myself dead, lying there in a coffin, but not insensate, not without feeling, not without a working mind. My body must have betrayed my discomfort. I looked up and read mirth in his eyes. I could see that he intended to make death something more than a specter.

We were interrupted at that moment by aides coming to take us to our baths.

"Federico, if you wish, we will continue this topic later."

I nodded assent, my mind numb. We never talked again. He became ill and his death three days later left me grief-stricken and bewildered. Where had he intended to lead me? Was it in his power to help me be at home with the death I have refused to look at? He had sent me into an unsettled territory, a swamp in which I might founder. Partially it is in respect for his memory, but more out of a personal compulsion, that I set out now to work myself free of this mire. I am forced to face what I have avoided facing, my own proximate death. What does *at home* mean?

The funeral is concluded. I hear the shuffle of old men on their way out. The choir is heavenly.

CHAPTER TWO

JOURNAL - May 6

In the sleepless hours before dawn this morning, my need to unscramble the confusion in my life pressed on me. The thought came to begin this journal to sort things out.

This apartment feels desolate now that Francis is gone. His wit and friendship made me feel comfortable here, but never at home. I was a guest and felt it, though not for lack of welcome. I will not be permitted to retain this apartment. It is much too spacious for one of my rank. It is papal in status. So, it is only a matter of time before the powers right this disarray in the pecking order. Then I will be like the Boll Weevil of song. I too will be "lookin' for a home."

Francis was the source of my self-knowledge. Knowing him, I learned my deficiencies. He was the mirror in which I saw a self I would be if I could. I learned from him that I need others to know myself, others to teach me how to leave my lesser self behind, others to loan me the courage to grow. Now I feel cryonic, frozen in time until others' warmth might thaw and open me that I might still flourish.

I will not stay in the Vatican. Rome? Perhaps. I realize now that I have never experienced the inner comfort of feeling at home in these one hundred-ten acres. Working for Francis, I did not fully experience the present. My focus was always on the future, on what we were working toward, toward a church as he envisioned it. Neither Francis nor his successor, Francis II, held office long enough to moderate the monarchical court structure and atmosphere that permeates every chapel, hall and man here. Such a place can be home only to the man at the top.

When Francis II died unexpectedly some six months ago, Cardinal Gervase Janov, president of the Pontifical Council for Promoting Christian Unity, was elected his successor. It was commonly expected that he would continue the reforms of the two Francises'. He had campaigned, in the oblique manner of clerics, on that promise. Once elected, however, he immediately set alarms ringing among reform-minded Catholics by taking the name, Innocent XIV. Despite his assurances that he only wished to restore eminence to a name whose early holders were among the most despotic of medieval popes, his actions since have created even greater concern.

My friends have told me how the trappings of court life are once again gaining favor among the prelates here in the Vatican. The near apotheosis of men who should use servant titles is evident in the rising use of Your Grace, Excellency, Eminence, and Holiness. Divine Rights are being theologized. Ornate clothing and conspicuous jewelry once again are signs of assumed status and greatness. My friends saw a return of the fear in their colleagues to speak out with their own unique voices. They noted the presence again of the dehumanizing sycophancy that court life demands, and witnessed the discontent and cynicism of men whose ambitions have been thwarted by circumstance of time, opportunity or death of a patron. Thank God they still saw some good, dedicated men unspoiled by ambition.

Now, but for one, my friends are gone from here and see these things from a distance. Claude Dupuis, our former Secretary of State, was retired against his wishes. He now lives in his native Provence. Tim Burns and Francis Ibowale have both been pushed upstairs and out, Tim to Glasgow and Francis to Nairobi. We write frequently, but it is not the same. Only Maggie remains in Rome and is now my sole confidant.

JOURNAL - May 7

I have too often been misdirected by assumptions, those that flow from my natural constitution and those from my training. In the consideration of my discomfort with death, these had best be examined carefully. I take it as an axiom that the good person, the holy person would be at home with death. If you were to ask me, "Are you a good person, a holy person?" I would be obliged to confess ignorance. What makes a person good? My concept of goodness has always been tied to obedience and loyalty to this church institution. That idea crumbled under the tutelage of Francis I. There are more fundamental loyalties, and I am no longer at home in my former beliefs.

What are the central truths of religion? I feel that my former vision is being challenged by what I learned from Francis I, and by what is now going on around me. I must review my most fundamental values, change them if necessary, to be at home with my Maker and with what should be my earthly response to the Divine design. My values and response must be dictated by my own conscience, not by ones given by dictate.

JOURNAL - May 8

As I reflect on my state I note a second defect. Not only am I not at home with my values and beliefs, but I am not at home in my own skin.

By the chance of ancestry I was gifted with the usual number of digits, greater appendages and organs. My mind was to prove more than adequate to my studies. My memory was perhaps my greatest boon, having always a greater problem to forget than to remember. If I lacked anything from my genetic pool it was confidence. The gauge of my supply seemed constantly in the red zone. Anxiety was my constant companion.

This is not a condition for which I assign blame to anyone. My mother was a berth of tranquility. My earliest memory of her, perhaps because of the event's frequent repetition, is in the kitchen of our row house on Monroe Street. My mother is baking, working the dough on the flour-sprinkled, white enamel top of our kitchen table. I sit at the table. The room is fragrant with the comfort odor of baking bread. There is a buttered crust on the table for me. I pick it up and point it up to trace the recessed squares of the butter-cream tin ceiling, and then down at those of the gray-green pattern on the worn linoleum floor. Before taking a bite I aim my crust at the round cylindrical motor that sits astride and powers the Frigidaire in the far corner. Mother sifts her flour with care, almost tenderness, and talks to me with words, the tenderness of which is what I remember.

And now I sift, filling my sieve first with these memories and slowly shaking them down and through, looking at them for relishment -- and for answers.

Memories of mother sift through in fine particles. Her name was Hilda, and she was beautiful, as all mothers are I suppose. Her rich brown hair was rolled back into a bun, in the same style her mother wore. The hair grayed over time, but the bun was always the same. Her eyes were blue, a deep sky blue and they looked out on the world with serious caring and a constant smile.

She was also a saint, something to which I would attest possibly whether it were true or not. However, she was a saint also to those of our neighborhood and St. Bridgid's parish. To my certain knowledge she never turned down a request for assistance. She raised money for any cause, baked breads, pies and cookies by the baker's dozens for every church bazaar. She helped out in the school lunch program, and in the school library. She was my father's perfect complement, he a ward politician, she his ever present faithful partner. She did the grunt work, the mailings, visits to the sick, chicken soup to the ailing, a mother confessor throughout the ward.

To me, she was a refuge from every anxiety. I could run to her and always find succor, if not in hugs, then always in jam and rolls -- in the manner of her own parents.

If my mother was complement to my father, he was also to her. Loquatious, Patrick Daniel Sweeney's smile started in his eyes and spread. He was a good man, if you know the drift of that phrase, a good provider, alert ever to the physical needs of his spouse and his two children. He loved my mother who was naturally quiet and submissive. And he loved his children, expecting in them those same qualities.

Father was the storyteller. At the evening dinner table he regaled us daily with the glories of his day. His stories were for the most part recounts of his verbal sparrings and his verbal victories. He had wit, and he retained its quickness in the heat of battle. The image came easily to us of this tall, thin, regally maned orator slaying his enemies with the sword of his tongue. The most potent weapon ever pointed at my father was a hammer in his own hands. He had no skill with repairs, only at talk. But he could coax laughter from the pursed face of Millie O'Connell and from the radiating-gloom countenance of Sister Mary Maud.

When I was in the sixth grade my father decreed that I should learn the fiddle. Despite my distaste for the idea I lacked the nerve to oppose him.

"You'll be grateful all the days of your life," he assured me. "And you will be prepared for the sounds of paradise." To Patrick Daniel an Irish air played lively by a fiddle, with soft thunder from a bodhran in the background, was the elevator music of heaven. The torture ended mercifully a year later when my instructor informed my father of my utter lack of musical talent. The instructor's report that I had nonetheless made a valiant try assuaged my father's mind, and spared me any further musical assignments.

My sister, Mary Colleen, two years older than myself, gave the first challenge ever to my father's authority. It happened on her graduation day, a bright blue day. Mother had invited a houseful of grandparents, aunts, uncles, cousins and neighbors for the celebration. Basking in the light of all that approval, Mary announced with enthusiasm that she planned to go to college with the expectation of becoming a physician.

"Oh, but that's a man's world, Mary," my father said, not unkindly.

"But it ought not be so," Mary replied.

"If it's medicine you want," he said, "you should consider the nursing profession."

"No, I'm good enough to be a doctor."

"I said nurse, Mary," he responded with quiet finality.

The joy of the day died. I avoided the fray, my sense of injustice swallowed under the pressure of anxiety.

Mary Colleen's final word came at the end of that summer when she eloped with Cormac Monaghan, an Irishman to be sure, but orange and Protestant. All such were slugabeds to Patrick Daniel Sweeney. It took a grandchild, another Patrick Daniel, to begin the mending.

My father's intrusion into Mary's career plans did not repeat itself when, in my senior year, I announced with trepidation that I had decided to enter the seminary. I recall directing the statement at my father, but with only a sidelong glance to catch his reaction. He blanched, coughed and was about to reply when my mother's delight could not be contained.

"Oh, that's wonderful," she exclaimed. "I've prayed so hard."

My father coughed again, and muttered only, "It's a decision to be made very carefully, Frederick." In private he was later to add only, "It is, I think, much easier to gain salvation as a lay person." Father was devout enough, but not a great fan of the clergy.

There is one thing, though, about anxiety. Unable to reach down for confidence, I somehow harnessed my fear in its place. Refusing slavery to it, I turned it into the motivation that pushed me to my successes, the academic hurdles, even eventually meeting the demands of necessary socialization. Apprehension became the propellant in my tank. I feared the journey, but I feared failure even more. With anxiety filling my sails I came to achieve every significant goal I set for myself.

Now at age sixty-one I discover myself rootless, soon to be without this physical shelter, adrift from my own self and from my convictions, floating in an unsound body on a fast track toward death. To resolve all these disparate conditions of self into a home is the reason I peck away at this computer.

I am the Waste Land of T. S. Eliot, a man who has led a sincere but inauthentic life. When I put my own self together, I will find home. I have a quest. I seek the Holy Grail, a man at peace with himself. I am compelled to re-examine everything. And I'm excited!

JOURNAL - May 9

I received my eviction notice in today's mail, a letter from Cardinal Mario Buongiorno, whose office oversees this apostolic palace. He didn't waste time.

Your Excellency:

Our departed Pontiff, Francis I, has shared his quarters in the apostolic palace with you these past few years. You will understand, I'm sure, that your rank of archbishop is not such that will permit you to continue in a papal apartment.

Accordingly, I am advising you to look for other lodgings at your earliest convenience. I suggest that the monastery of St. Alcuin near Viterbo might interest you. Abbot Joachim is most hospitable and would welcome you. The ambiance there is one of rustic beauty, an atmosphere well suited to meditation in one's final days.

Cordially,

+ Card. Mario Buongiorno

I will leave, of course, but not to a monastery, even one of rustic beauty. I am accustomed to a small measure of comfort, and the idea of a monk's cell is not inviting. Moreover, I have always been an urban man. I would not find a vista of grazing and cud-chewing cows conducive to sanity, much less meditation.

***

I am unable to be sad or anxious in Maggie's presence. I confess my spirit sagged on receiving the eviction notice. I fight this tendency to anxiety, but sometimes fail. Maggie is always a tonic. Her visit today has returned my preoccupations to happier vistas. We will, she suggested, find a place where she can supervise my care. Frankly, I am elated by the prospect.

My sister, Mary Colleen, invited me to live with her and her family in Chicago. She is a generous, caring woman, but duty resounds in her invitation. I would not be at home there. I do not wish to be a burden to anyone until that is all I can be. Maggie's suggestion seems devoid of burden. Is that Maggie's way, or my wish?

Maggie is Sister Margaret McDonough, President of the Congregation for Justice. We are friends, but it was not always so. I first became acquainted with her when she was president of Padua College in Mill Valley, Wisconsin, and I was the bishop of that diocese. In a speech delivered in Denver she accused the bishops of conspiracy in the suppression of women. She was correct, but I didn't see it at the time, and bristled at such an insinuation. The feeling of shame fills me at the memory of how I successfully intrigued with her board of trustees to oust her from the presidency. It appalls me now how I so unwittingly assumed that my decision reflected the mind and will of the Deity.

It took the murder of one of my priests to bring me to my senses. He was killed by a young man who had been abused by another priest, but who in deranged confusion shot this innocent one. I had failed both the boy and the priest. Through that event I came to see clearly that it is a bishop's role to be servant to the people, not to an institution, and to welcome and listen carefully to dissent.

Eventually I sought Maggie out to apologize. That scene, in her office at Highmount College in New York, where she had been selected as president, remains vivid, and uncomfortable.

"It was kind of you to come, Bishop," she said, a chill in her voice. "For what it's worth, I accept your apology."

Her words were welcome, but the cold reserve with which she responded was a replica of what my own had been toward her. I deserved it.

I was later invited to the Vatican to work with my mentor, Cardinal Alberto della Tevere. He had formed a group he called *Il Cero,* the candle, to review all the structures of the church. Alberto was the first to recognize a vacuum in our group. We had no woman member and so were lacking in female competence and perspective. He asked each member to recommend someone. From a feeling of guilt perhaps, but also because I knew she would be an honest broker for women, I recommended Maggie. Alberto invited her to Rome to talk. She came. They talked. He invited her to join *Il Cero.* He persuaded her to join us, despite her evident animosity toward me.

The saying that time heals may be a cliche, but time is nonetheless an effective therapist. Maggie and I came to know each other's mind and heart. We became friends and have remained so over these years.

When Alberto was elected Pope, he founded the Congregation for Justice, and appointed Maggie to be its president.

She had been the *Il Cero* member who clearly demonstrated the need to provide a forum where even the poorest could resolve their complaints of injustice against bishops, even against the Curia.

Perhaps that is why she was exceptionally animated today. Two days from now she will hold court and will hand down a number of decisions, one of which involves no less an eminent defendant than the Vatican Secretary of State, Cardinal Juan Oliva. He is a close confidant of Pope Innocent. This closeness and the power between them raises anxiety in me for Maggie. I told her that. She shushed me. She is fearless.

Still, I intuit danger for her. We will reconvene on the matter of my future abode when she has completed her day in court.

CHAPTER THREE

Maggie walked from the shadowed street of her apartment into the morning brightness of the *Piazza Campo di Fiori.* Vendors were filling their stalls with displays of fresh foodstuff and brilliant flowers. A few brisk steps took her inside Mario Cassini's establishment, a pinched space in an ancient building adjoining the piazza. "Good morning, Mario."

"Good morning, Sister Maggie," the proprietor replied. "A beautiful day is it not?" He wiped his hands on a spotless white apron.

"It augurs well, Mario," Maggie said, voicing a wish for the day ahead.

"Yes, yes, yes. And what is your desire this morning, Sister?"

"Is the pastry fresh today, Mario?" she began a familiar routine.

"But of course it is fresh. I make it myself only this morning."

"Good. I'll have one of those." She pointed at a pear-centered pastry. "And the milk, Mario? Is the milk fresh?"

"I milk the cow on my way to work, Sister. But, what is this, no caffe espresso today?"

"No. I'll have milk. I'm wired enough."

"Nervous, Sister? You?"

"No, just excited." Maggie paid the bill. "Ciao, Mario."

"Ciao, Sister."

She munched her pastry as she walked a back street to the *Corso Vittorio Emanuele.* There, waiting for the #62 bus, she crumbled the waxed-paper pastry grip and stuck it in her briefcase. She opened the small carton of milk, her thoughts on the day ahead. She wondered if Cardinal Oliva would personally appear in court today.

The bus was crowded but a red-faced young cleric rose quickly to give her his seat. Strange, she thought. That's a first. She thanked him and took the seat. The reason for his blush was immediately apparent. Next to her a young mother had pulled up her blouse just enough to give a breast to her baby, and was unabashedly stroking the milk supply toward the nipple. Looking up at the embarrassed cleric Maggie wondered if he felt compelled to rush to a confessional. To make sin of what is so natural, how strange these clerics are. And how strange not to make sin of what Cardinal Oliva tries to defend. "You have a beautiful baby," she said to the mother. "Is it a girl or a boy?"

"It is a boy, Sister. His name is Roberto. My first baby."

"He is perfect," Maggie said. "You are a fortunate young woman."

The bus crossed the Tiber and she exited at the *Via della Conciliazione* stop. Looking up the street's wide expanse at St. Peter's Basilica, she said a silent prayer for the day, for the decisions she would hand down. To be publicly reprimanded for his policies in the Caribbean, or for any policy will be a first for the Secretary of State. Thinking a prayer for Cardinal Oliva and for his diplomatic staff, she stopped to check her appearance in the window of a bank. She fretted briefly on the increasing salt and pepper look of her hair, and centered the silver medalion of her religious order on the jacket of her tailored navy suit. She must remember to put it over her judicial robe for the court session.

She walked the few blocks to where the street ended in St. Peter's Square, turned right and entered a building that faced the Basilica. Seconds later she emerged from an elevator on the third floor, fumbling in her purse for a key.

She did not notice the Swiss Guard who stood by the door of the department.

"E chiuso, Senora," he said, turning her way. Then he recognized her. "It is closed, Sister Maggie."

"Oh, hi Kurt. I didn't see you. It's okay. I have the key." She held it up.

"No, Sister. It is closed. It is forbidden for anyone to enter. I have these orders."

"Why? Is there some danger in the building, Kurt?"

"No, Sister."

Stunned, she asked, "Who gave you this order, Kurt?"

"My superior, Sister. He called me early this morning and directed me to start my shift early. Here, at this location, with those instructions."

She felt her heart thump. "I'll check on it. Thanks, Kurt."

At the entrance to the building her deputy, Bishop Peter Van Antwerpen, hurtled through the door and they nearly collided. The usually calm face of the stumpy, bespectacled Peter held a crazed expression. "Look!" he said. "Have you seen this?" He held out a newspaper, the day's edition of *L'Osservatore Romano,* and opened it to the section heading, *Nostre Informazioni.* He pointed to a small, unheadlined blurb.

She took the paper and read:

> *His Holiness, Pope Innocent XIV, has suppressed the curia's Congregation for Justice. In an Apostolic Brief, Justitia Beatissima, the pontiff explains that the Congregation was hastily initiated several years ago. Subsequent study indicates that all of the rights of the faithful can*

> *be affirmed, adjudicated and protected by judicial forums already in place. Morevover, economy requires that we consolidate...*

Maggie's eyes blazed. "Peter, catch all the staff as they come in. Have them bring any documents, investigations, CD's, and records of any kind in their possession to the Trattoria San Stefano. We'll meet there at 11:00 this morning. Set it up, please."

Peter nodded.

Maggie took a deep breath to let her heart slow down, and then pushed through the door. A Mercedes limo sat at the curb. Behind a back window the eyes of Cardinal Juan Oliva stared directly at her. She held his stare. Then he spoke to his driver and the limo pulled away. She walked the short distance to the Vatican and entered the apostolic palace. At Fred's apartment she pushed the doorbell insistently. She knew it took him time to work the remote for the latch and waited, tapping a foot. When the lock clicked she rushed in.

"I need to use your phone, Fred."

"Help yourself." He read the distress in her face as she dialed.

"This is Sister Margaret McDonough. It is urgent that I speak with His Holiness. He's busy? No. No. I insist that I speak to him. Ask him, please? What do you mean, he doesn't choose to speak to me? Oh..."

Fred saw dejection spread over her face.

She looked at him. "I'll try his gatekeeper." She dialed again, introduced herself, and said, "May I speak with Cardinal Buongiorno, please? It is important. Yes, I'll wait." She glanced at Fred, her eyes raised in total exasperation. "Your Eminence, thank you for taking my call. I urgently need an appointment with His Holiness. Is there an opening? Yes, I'll wait." She fumbled a pen from her purse.

"You're not serious? Nothing until September? Four months? No, no thank you." She hung up. "Bastards," she muttered. Then, "Sorry, Fred."

"What is it, Maggie?" he asked. "What's this all about?"

"They've suppressed my department, Fred. The Congregation for Justice is history. Here, read it." She put *L'Osservatore Romano* on the table in front of him. "I've got to get my staff together. I'll see you when I've sorted this out."

***

"Sister Maggie, hold up." The voice came from behind her as she left the apostolic palace. She turned. "Hello, Henri."

Monsignor Henri Helpre of the Secretariat of State came alongside puffing. "I thought I saw you pass the office," he said. "Catching you now will save me a search later. I'm directed to give you this letter." He handed her an envelope embossed with the seal of the Secretariat. "Sorry about Justice going down." He looked sorry, like he wanted to talk.

"Thanks, Henri. I've got to run now. An appointment." In the taxi she instructed the driver. "Piazza Navona, please," and opened the envelope.

Dear Sister McDonough:

I am directed by His Holiness to send you the following instructions in regard to the suppression of the Department of Justice.

I. Under obedience to His Holiness neither you nor any member of your staff are to make public comment, oral or written, regarding the suppression.

II. Under penalty of automatic (Latae sententiae) excommunication you and each member of your staff are required to deliver to this Secretariat within three days any and all Department of Justice materials and records of any kind that may be in your possession.

III. An oath of compliance is enclosed. You are to have a sufficient number copied for your staff, but no more. You and your staff are each required to sign the oath and return it to me at the Secretariate within forty-eight hours.

By the explicit authority vested in me by His Holiness, Innocent XIV

+ Cardinal Juan Oliva

Maggie let her body fall back into the seat and rested her head against the cushion. Her feelings invited a disturbing memory, her imprisonment in Central America.

Soon after the Congregation for Justice had been established, she had gone there to investigate the murder of three nuns and a bishop. She again saw her prison cell, about six by twelve feet. The cement-block walls and concrete floor were wet, as if someone had hosed them down. They were stained with brownish blotches. The door was solid metal except for a four- inch window. A squat toilet sat at the back wall. It had a dark crack, a jagged wound in its side. A scum-coated sink clung to the wall next to the toilet. The narrow, board bunk, its outer edge held by heavy chains, was hinged to the wall.

She recalled the thrust of the door as it swung open, and the strut of an officer named Molina. "Hello, bitch," he muttered. "How would you like to feel the Sierra Madre rumble?" He reached out and slapped her violently across the face, then grabbed her by the shoulders.

In her memory, Maggie struggled, striking back without effect. "No! Don't!" she shouted at him.

A cruel smile contorted Molina's face. "Good, bitch. Fight back! Fight!" he goaded. He grabbed her by her hair and swung her from wall to wall with one hand, gouging and punching with the other. Maggie's grunts of pain turned into screams. Her screams only broadened the savage grin on Molina's face. Then he stopped the beating and, piece by piece, tore away her clothes. He threw her, naked, to the cell floor and covered her with his heavy body. His knuckles poked and prodded at her face, her eyes, her ears.

She found herself suddenly outside her body, detached, and looking down on the attack. Her breathing was rapid and shallow as she watched Molina's arms flail downward, the forced spread of her legs, and the pounding thrusts of his body.

Maggie felt sweat breaking out and wrenched her mind away from the scene. She had been rescued from the prison, but it took months before she was freed from denial and depression. The feeling of violation is the same today, she thought as the taxi worked its way free of a traffic jam. Rape comes in many forms. Only this time there will be no denial, no depression. This time all the people have been raped. The bastards!

Her staff of eleven was already assembled in a private room of the Trattoria San Stefano when she arrived. She started the meeting by telling them of her failed attempts to reach the pontiff. "We can't delude ourselves that this suppression can be reversed. We are up against an absolute power who did not consult us beforehand, and now refuses to even meet with us. So, no illusions, please." Then she read Oliva's letter. Looking around the table she saw the disgust registered on each face. She asked nevertheless. "Does anyone want a copy of the compliance oath?"

Everyone raised turned-down thumbs.

"I knew that would be your response. Now, where do we go from here? I want your thoughts."

"The story has to be told," Peter said, a sentiment that received ayes all around the table.

"But the story can't be told if we can't get to our documentation," one investigator, Eileen, said. "From the locked office and the oath of compliance it's clear that those behind this suppression want our documentation to disappear. We can't let that happen. They already control one set of our records, those at the office.

Peter took a key from his pocket. "We still have access to the back-ups in the bank. Eileen, you and Pat, take off right now and get them, make two copies, and return the back-ups to the safe deposit box."

Maggie pulled a diskette from her purse. "This is the final diskette. Copy it too, please."

"If any of you have documents or investigative materials that have not yet been digitized, get them to me," Peter directed. "I suggest that I personally take one set of records to a secure place in the Netherlands."

"Can you set up a web site there, one where we will all have easy, but secure access?" Maggie asked.

"Can do," Peter replied.

"Eileen, please mail one set to me c/o Sister Felicity Matthews at my motherhouse. Here's the address." She handed over a business card. "Be sure to use the Italian mail service, not the Vatican's."

"They can shut us down, but they're not going to shut us up," Peter said, a measure of exuberance in his voice now. "Rome has no place for us now. They can disperse us, but they can't cut our communication."

Maggie looked around the table slowly, meeting each person's eyes. Tears began to flood her eyes and her voice was low and trembly. "I have not been informed, but I suspect that our individual compensation ended with the suppression. I wish I had the power to find secure employment for each of you. I don't. But I know you and I know your competence. You will not only survive, you will thrive. You are a great team and I could never adequately express my esteem for each of you. Our remaining time together will be short, but we will meet here every day at this time. We will fight in the only way left to us. We will expose what has happened for the world to see." She stood up. "Right now, I need a hug from each of you."

***

Maggie entered her apartment later that day to find the light on her telephone message system flashing. She punched the button.

"Maggie, it's Felicity. Call me. Important."

"My God, they're trying to control me through my religious superior back home, Maggie thought, then smiled. They don't know Felicity. She dialed the motherhouse.

"I've been directed by the Congregation for Religious to put a muzzle on you, dear," Felicity said. "They came down hard with the obedience stick. I told them that obedience is a much over-rated virtue, and something other than a virtue if used for repression. Of course, dear, I tried to couch it in Vaticanese. You should know, Maggie, that every single sister of yours has expressed her support for you. Do what you have to do."

"Thanks, Felicity. It's nice to know my back is covered and I have a home waiting. What's this I hear about you retiring?"

"It's true, dear. And now it seems, as the saying goes, you have occasioned my finest hour in office. Thank you. You take care, and remember how precious you are to all of us."

"Thanks. Oh, Felicity. Lots of records coming your way. Protect them, okay?"

"Will do, dear. Bye."

Maggie stayed at her apartment the rest of the day. She wanted to think, to plan. But the phone kept ringing, her staff, the curious, the press, friends. Late in the evening she had a call from Shelly Burg, a friend back in Wisconsin. They talked for an hour. In bed, she wept herself to sleep.

CHAPTER FOUR

It would feel so good right now to punch a pillow -- or a prelate. How does a man with no physical muscle vent his bile? I was speechless with anger before Maggie was out the door. I read the newspaper report of the suppression of her department.

The story behind the suppression is the sad story of the Arawaki island nation. The history of Arawaki and its Caribbean island natives have been much in the press over the past decade. The natives have always been poor. Like their peers of Central America they have been padlocked for centuries to their poverty, exploited by the power and collusion of the few. Efforts by these disfranchised natives to improve their lot have been consistently and viciously repressed. Tens of thousands have been killed.

I recall how an occasional priest would speak out, but they too were either killed or expelled. The bishops lacked either the conscience or the courage to be voices for the poor, and instead allied themselves with the elite. They hid behind the shallow rationalization that every attempt at simple justice was a cover for communism. In the last decade the poor finally found a voice in the person of a courageous priest called Vicente. He became their leader. Headlines come back to me of how he was condemned by the government, hunted by the secret police, expelled from his own religious order, and slandered by the bishops and the CIA as unstable. Still, he continued preaching against the oppression.

I remember front-page descriptions of how the elite oligarchy, pressured to hold an election, were flabbergasted when their candidate was buried under a landslide of votes for the priest. Headlines soon followed of a coup sponsored by the elite, the Vatican, the bishops and the CIA, which overthrew that legitimately elected government. Buried in the back pages was a report that the Vatican, in the person of Cardinal Oliva, rushed to be the first to give official recognition to the coup government, recognition that it had denied the legitimately elected priest.

Maggie told me of the overthrown government's appeal to have her department overturn Oliva's action. Fill in the blanks: Maggie's staff investigated, found against Oliva, decision to be announced today, Oliva does an end run.

I fear for Maggie and imagine her feelings. I know her personal history and can feel her sense of violation. Only this time the violence came not from an enemy, but from those who should be her supporters. Maggie has many friends here, but no longer any with power. She knows the guards, the postal employees, the vendors, all by first name, but is not invited to the meetings where power is represented. To her credit, but against my advice, she has not marketed herself to the powerholders in the way bureaucrats do, by alliances, favors, remembrances. She held the illusion that here, where love is preached to be the cement that binds us together, competence would be enough to protect her. Her idealism is most endearing, but of little protection in an institution where power poses as authority, and authority serves power instead of people.

***

I didn't sleep. I obsess on Maggie and her plight. My spleen overflows and floods my brain. I tried to call the pope, but received the same purposeful silence that Maggie got. Like Maggie I tried for an appointment, and failed. I called Cardinal Oliva and he took the call. He met my advocacy for the Congregation of Justice with rude and abrupt dismissal. I have no more power here than does the most illiterate peasant in the most remote region of the world.

But I have learned something. I have experienced what the poor of this world experience daily. Helplessness. To that extent at least, I am now more their brother. It is an unpleasant lesson, but not a bad one I think.

The Roman Curia, the pope's administrative arm, is commonly referred to as *The Holy See*. I wonder where the *holy* is. Is it hidden somewhere behind the secrecy and fog-bound spin of diplomatic chatter? Does it lurk somewhere in the repression of so many honest seekers of truth and justice, in the suppression of theologians, movements, and now even a curial department? Such power displays, and forced prostrations of even their most loyal members, give credence to the thesis that they provide sexual release for this Holy See's celibate masters.

I am too full of bile. I must go pray.

***

Maggie spent the morning with me. She drained my spleen and banished my melancholy over coffee and muffins. Less than two weeks after the suppression of her department, she is full of optimism. Defeat transformed into opportunity. She moves forward and says to look back is a waste of energy. She is going back to the States. Midwestern University outside of Chicago called with an offer to join its history department. They want her to write the history of the Congregation of Justice.

"I think the hand of God is in this, Fred," she said. "What an exceptional opportunity to do what I have to do, expose that bit of history. I'll teach one course on papal history and the rest of my time can go to research and to writing."

I was pleased for her, but my heart pained at the thought of her absence. Would she first park me in some nursing home? She had promised to help me find a place to live, and she keeps her word.

"I've been planning this with Shelly Burg. She and her husband, Bill and their two young sons, live in a small village called Plum. You remember Shelly. You met her when they visited me."

I nodded. I do remember Shelly, a pert, independent-thinking strawberry blond.

"Shelly helped me set this whole thing up."

"I can't believe you put this all together so fast."

"Just good luck, Fred. Besides, I'm a realist. I knew when they took my congregation down that it's over for me here. You knew it too."

I wanted to take her hand. "You're a dear, dear friend, Maggie. I'll miss you terribly. But it is the perfect answer for you. I'm happy for you."

"Don't be silly, Fred. You're coming too. Unless you choose not to. Shelly has found a large home for us in Plum, one that will accommodate your needs. There's a commuter to the University. And Felicity has offered to join us. She's retiring you know. She will manage the household, help in my research, and," mischief in her voice, " help me keep an eye on you. Also, there's a wonderful doctor in Plum, Shelly says. Her name is Robyn Horsager. She'll oversee your care."

"She?"

"Fred? Does that embarrass you?"

"I can handle it." I hoped I could handle it.

"Good. It's settled then?"

"Will I be looking at cows all day?"

"No, but a little more time with cows might loosen you up." She was laughing.

"Watching a cow lazily chew its cud could be a lessen in meditation, like watching a carrot wilt. Besides, Chicago is just a hop, skip away. You can visit your sister and family when you wish. Most important, we will live close to people, *real* people."

I hesitated, knowing what a burden I would be to her. Fortunately, I remembered a lesson learned long ago. There are two sides to love of neighbor, the giving side and the receiving side. There is a compulsion in me to think only of the giving side, though I'm not sure what that means. I must learn. It is my time to receive. I have no alternative. And who better to receive from than someone who has offered to be the giver, a friend.

"Well," she said, "Are you coming?"

How could I refuse? We leave Rome in three days, on the first of June.

JOURNAL - June 3

We are at sea, our second full day in a voyage of six days. It is a sun-filled tranquil day. Maggie sits in a lounge chair next to me, reading Kristin Lavransdatter, *her lifetime favorite for the third time. My wheelchair is secured in place by blocks at the wheels. The laptop rests lightly on my legs.*

I do not know if it is a desirable skill, but I have the ability to tune out the world around me. Today it works well for me. I have watched and listened to the sea long enough to let its magic work in the background of my experiencing.

Where do I begin in my search for tranquility? I must find peace in my beliefs, in my own skin, and with the death that I feel rushing at me. Where else but at the beginning. It is my confident intuition that if I find peace in my beliefs and values, the others will follow.

There are times when I feel lost in the forest of countless spiritualities, devotions and traditional practices of my faith. There must exist a source, a root from whence they spring, and by which they can be judged and given a value.

That root can only be God and God's love for his creation. Everything begins there. And when that love turns toward humankind it grows to a passion. I believe that God is crazy about us, each of us. It has taken me a lifetime to rid myself of the cruel, avenging, punishing, hellfire-threatening God instilled in me as a child. That God is not dead for everyone, but the truth is that such a God does not exist. Isn't it some species of blasphemy to paint attributes on God that we would find unacceptable in our next door neighbor?

How did I arrive at this root truth? How does a person look through the everyday tragedies that surround us and find a loving God? I sense how difficult it must be for many people to find a God of love through the prism of pain, suffering and privation. But I believe they will find that God if they listen quietly. My root truth is based on the belief that Jesus was, in his life and in his dying, the revelation of the character of God. Jesus did not die on a cross to ransom us from the devil, as the metaphor of St. Paul would have it. Nor did Jesus die to satisfy some demand of justice on God's part as retribution for sin, as theologies from the eleventh century onward would posit. The sole mission that Jesus had was to show God to us.

He was an intimate of God. He called God Abba, Daddy. He said to his apostle, Phillip, "If you see me, Phillip, you see the Father."

What God exists behind what we see in Jesus? He loved his neighbors, and they included the outcasts, the untouchables, the maimed, foreigners, prostitutes, rogues, tax collectors, and the invisible of his time, women. He healed anyone who needed healing. More important, he ate and drank with them. He lived at their level. For his efforts and for directing religious expression away from laws and ritual, he became a threat to the religious leaders and their privileged status. They had him killed. So, for loving others he died, and in dying showed the full passion of God for us.

It is not possible for a human to comprehend a love greater than that of one who lays down his or her life for another. But that is exactly what Jesus did in his living and in the dying it led to. His death shows us a God who, in terms of human understanding, is someone who lays down His life for us. God is Someone who loves each of us to the limit of our ability to understand what love is.

That's the Gospel! That's the Good News! That's the rock core of my beliefs!

JOURNAL - June 5

I love the lazy roll of the ship in these calm seas. I suspect the pace of this crossing will help us adjust to the pace in Plum. The day drags so I return to my thoughts.

After revealing God as one who loves us unconditionally, Jesus invites us to love God in return by loving our neighbor. "By this will all men know you are my disciples, that you love one another." Love of neighbor is not a command hurled at us from above. It is law only because, written in our hearts, it says: if you would be yourself, your best self, love your neighbor. Instinctively, we know this to be true. Throughout all of our history mankind has recognized instinctively that the hero or saint, the best anyone can be, is someone who puts his or her life on the line for others. True religious response to God calls for nothing more than putting ourselves on track to become our best selves. I can shout praise, yell love, shoot cannons, ring bells, burn incense, and clang cymbals all I want, but I can only show love to God by loving people.

But how do I do that? I fear this ALS is less a disability than the one I have in loving others. Will Plum and its people teach me the how of it? I think it my last chance.

CHAPTER FIVE

We are settled in Plum, a village of about five hundred in the Southeast corner of Wisconsin. The village is a garden of homes set on green, tree laden lawns and abuts a wide lazy river. Plum is situated about fifteen miles from the county seat of Stockford on a direct line to Chicago, an equal distance beyond. Midwestern University is located in Stockford, so Maggie will have that commute. Our home is a large Carpenter Gothic, once the pride of a wealthy lumber magnate.

I am lodged on the first floor where I enjoy a bedroom and a spacious study whose windows look down over the town and the river beyond. Not a cow in sight. All my life I have been an urban creature, accustomed to city clamor. I am not accustomed to the quiet I find here, but it lends itself wonderfully to meditation and to writing. I am filled with serene and good feelings.

And I have a new vehicle, a four-wheeled scooter that gives me access to this entire floor and to the sidewalk and street. It has a brace that holds my head erect. I've been testing it, edging to the table and to my desk and running it through open doors. The seat swivels and I can use it for either desk or table chair. The manual claims it can reach speeds of ten miles per hour. This afternoon I will take it outside and test its mettle. I call my shiny red speedster Rover, after a childhood tricycle over which I was equally excited.

Maggie tells me that her apartment is directly above mine and has the same roomy layout with bedroom and study. A third apartment upstairs will be occupied by Sister Felicity Matthews, a longtime friend of Maggie. Felicity has recently completed her last term as president of their religious order. She will manage our household, having told Maggie that she has been looking for just such an opportunity. I remember her well, and recall how the age lines of her face tumble upward into a fixed smile. She will arrive this coming Sunday.

An apartment above the garage will house a muscular and likable young man, Cory Smith. He is a physical therapist associated with Dr. Robyn Horsager here in Plum. Cory will aid me as needed to begin and end my days and to bathe. I can still manage my other personal needs, having sufficient strength in my arms to move from scooter to toilet.

***

Two days in Plum and already I have made something of a splash. On my test ride of Rover yesterday, I easily maneuvered through the house, and onto the driveway and street. I turned toward the downtown, only two blocks away. The street has a downward slope in that direction and I took advantage of it and opened the throttle to full speed. I went through the first intersection without slowing down. The freedom of it, the rush of fresh air! As I approached the village's main street I fully intended to slow down, but brain and muscle malfunctioned. I forgot that both brake and throttle are on the scooter arms and kept telling my useless right foot to brake, a muscle memory going back no doubt to my first car, a used 1962 Chevy.

I wheeled onto the main street and a beer truck screeched to a halt, stopping just short of me before I raced onto a ramp for launching boats. At this point I simply gave up and became a spectator. Picture my race to the water. We struck the river with force enough to slow the scooter and propel me over the steering handles into the river. Physically, I was uninjured. And my disease has begun to free me from my ego. So instead of burying myself in embarrassment, I enjoyed the swim. I'm happy to report that I can still float.

The water was warm and refreshing, but I was not permitted to enjoy it for long. Two muscular arms took hold of me, it seems within seconds, and I was hauled, toes out to sea, back to the ramp. I sat, legs outstretched, on the asphalt and watched my rescuing giant retrieve Rover.

I heard correctly, but asked for his name a second time just to be sure.

"Dumpster," he replied. "Dumpster Heap. I'm the constable here in Plum. Saw you whiz across the street and figured you were in trouble."

I thanked him for the rescue.

"Seems to me, your vehicle could use some drying out," he continued. "I'll let you sit on that bench up by the tracks while I take the scooter over to Jimmy's garage for a check. The sun will dry you soon enough."

He lifted me off the asphalt as if I had the weight of a child and carried me to the bench.

"Be right back," he said.

I felt the weight of my wet denims, my favorite uniform now, on my body. I sat on the bench and the sun had its way with me. I was warm, but not dry when he returned.

"There's better ways to go fishin'," he said. "Still, I'll have to check your license."

I started to explain that I wasn't fishing when I saw the clear glint of humor in his eyes. We both started laughing and for a long time I couldn't stop. I was taken by the freedom that laughter brings. Finally, I introduced myself.

"I already heard about you, sir. Welcome to Plum. It'll be a while before your vehicle is ready."

Dumpster is a good talker. He told me about Plum, a subject clearly to his liking. The river whch runs along the village is called the Badger. Train tracks run parallel and next to the river through the town. Inward from the tracks, Main Street, which is also a highway, fronts a business section several blocks long. A strange looking, flat-topped hill stands perhaps a third of a mile behind Main Street. Dumpster referred to it as *Uptop.* Three churches rest Uptop. Most of the homes in Plum lay below the hill and behind the string of stores and offices. Some straggled north or south and around the corners of the hill. According to the constable, the editor of the local newspaper had dubbed it the Fertile Crescent from the number of births he printed in his weekly.

Dumpster's love for the river was evident. From his descriptions I could almost see the ghosts of boatmen whose once busy traffic carried goods out to Lake Michigan and to the world beyond. They now had their thin reminders in the lazy flow of occasional fishermen. Their outboards and the infrequent rumble of freight or commuter trains were the sole irritant to a visitor's peace. Per Dumpster, local folks learned quickly to tune them out.

I was curious about the three churches Uptop, and asked Dumpster.

"Well," he said, "Some folks say that long, oval-shaped hill is a drumlin, a waste product of a drifting glacier. Personally, I don't think glaciers got this far south. Whatever the case, it sure is an oddity out here in the middle of a flat plain. Look how it's been shorn nearly flat. Don't have a clue how that happened.

"Of course, it being high, religions took to it. Those are Evangelical Lutheran Church in America, United Church of Christ, and Roman Catholic churches sitting up there, their fronts facing east. My Uncle Hiram told me that the land Uptop was once owned by a single family, name of O'Rourke, and was split among three sons on the death of the father. The sons didn't get along and made public their mutual dislike by joining three different churches. When one of them donated his Uptop acres to his church, the other boys did the same to their churches."

Listening to Dumpster, you'd think Plum was Camelot. His sense of responsibility for its citizens oozes out. For nearly an hour I was his student. But I was Fred, not sir, within two minutes. Dumpster is a man you can't help liking. He offered to drive me home, but I declined, savoring the sun and his descriptions. So, I've made my first friend here. He has promised to take me fishing so I'll learn how to do it "proper." And he'll visit me on his 'rounds.' I look forward to both.

***

Maggie and I attended Mass this Sunday morning at St. Anne's, Uptop. The pastor, Jack Tyrrell, is a youthful forty or so, with blond long hair that juts back into a rubber-banded ponytail. He did a good job on the liturgy and gave a good homily. Maggie and I introduced ourselves and shook hands, but had no time to talk in the rush of people.

Felicity arrived early this afternoon and took control. She is still a woman with a perpetual smile, ample in size, and has a ready wit. She assigned me garbage duty, lawn care, snow shoveling and general maintenance responsibilities, and then allowed that she might grant me specific absolutions dependent on good behavior. I'm going to like that lady.

"Should I address you as 'Your Grace?'" she asked.

"Only if you like the title 'Mother General,'" I replied.

"Fred?"

"Felicity?"

Laughter has been the dominating sound of the day. Right now it emanates from the kitchen, where she and Maggie are preparing dinner.

CHAPTER SIX

The living room, usually spic and span, was cluttered this evening. Stacks of photo albums rose from the floor. Cartons filled with trays of slides stood chest high to the left of his worn leather chair. He had set up a viewing screen in front of the fireplace and a projector on a table to the right of his chair's arm.

He began his viewing with the oldest of the albums, blowing dust from worn covers before turning to the photos. Tracing the photo history of his ancestors he flipped through the pages quite rapidly until he came to the albums whose portrayals brought personal remembrances, those that began with the second Chase generation, his grandparents, great aunts and great uncles, all dead by the time he reached his teens.

The pace of his review slowed even more as he read the faces of his parents and their siblings. He stopped and stared long at those photos that smiled back at him.

John Plum Chase would have been John William Chase IV except for the capricious gift of his middle name. The name Plum had drifted unused down the generations since John William Chase I had bestowed it as a loving nickname on his wife, and as its real name on the settlement that grew up around his general store. The store, long gone, had sat on the banks of the Badger and served both river traffic and settlers.

At age eighty, John had outlived his wife and his two sons, all three taken from him by colon cancer. A sole grandchild, another John William, had died in an auto crash. John was now the last Chase.

John's wealth was considerable, though not visible in this farm style home that had once been surrounded by fields of corn but was now set amidst lawns and houses. His wealth had come from past generations, added to by his own effort. It was the accumulation from corn that annually filled cribs from fifteen hundred acres of fertile soil. He had been a successful developer of hybrid seed corn that he grew and sold from his own and rented fields.

When he had reviewed all the albums, he turned to the slides, all of them of his generation. He began an unhurried progress through more than a hundred trays, stopping long at the smiling faces of Edna and the boys, John William and Henry. A photo of the boys in basketball uniform standing inside the gym trapped his memory. He had donated the gym to the high school. He had also donated the village library, and, as reminded by a smiling photo of Dumpster Heap, the combination firehouse and police station.

He was an excessively shy man and had not permitted the villagers to put his name on any of his donated buildings. Nor had he even allowed them to fete him personally at the events that celebrated each structure's completion. Everyone knew of his generosity, however, and felt a deep reverence toward him. They mistook his shyness for a privacy preference and honored it. He was never comfortable in small talk. His yes or no responses made for short conversations and long awkward silences. When he retired he was often invited to dinner at one home or another, but he always found a reason not to go, reasoning privately that the invitations were gracious responses for his gifts. It never occurred to him that they might indicate a desire for friendship. Eventually, the invitations ceased. Dumpster would stop by on occasion for a visit, but had to carry the brunt of any conversation. Jack Tyrrell visited occasionally in the hope of coaxing John back to active participation in the church. Wounds caused by a priest's arrogance somewhere in the past went too deep.

At two o'clock in the morning, halfway through the slide trays, John felt the need for food and turned off the projector. Walking to the kitchen, he recalled an item from the Chicago paper of the previous day. A condemned man, an Irishman, had requested corned beef and cabbage for his last meal. Pushing the thought away, John began to prepare his favorite treat, popcorn. He transferred the popped corn from the microwave popper to a large bowl and, in a slow, loving ritual, ladled melted butter onto it.

He carried the bowl of hullless white puffs, a napkin, and a cola to the living room, and resumed his viewing. Tray after tray helped him trace his own life and career, and he stopped every time a face beamed back at him. As each tray emerged he dropped it on the floor and took the next from ordered rows in a carton.

He finished the viewing and the popcorn as morning sun began to stream through the windows. He sat a moment in thought, looking at a crucifix on the wall. Then walking to a desk he returned with a pen and note pad. He scribbled a note, then reached for a revolver on the projector table and put the barrel into his mouth.

***

The small boat drifted with the sluggish current of Beef Slough. Dumpster dipped an oar to keep the craft on track with the shore. A flick of his fly rod sent the line curling toward the shallow shoreline water where spawning blue gills had cratered the pebbled bottom with their nests. Nearly every cast drew in a squirming, resistant blue. Dumpster measured each fish against his outsized hand. Roughly one in four met his standard to get tossed into a trolling bucket at the side of the boat. When the catch numbered enough for his dinner, and for that of Elaine Stubben, his elderly, widowed neighbor, he dropped an anchor, placed a flat pine board on his lap and proceeded to clean the fish. Two sweeps of his knife per side of fish yielded a fillet to slide onto ice in the cooler. The waste went back into the slough, protein for hungry predators.

Within minutes the cleaning was finished. He dipped the board into the slough and cleaned its surface with his palm. Stowing the board he wiped his hands dry on a piece of faded green towel. The sun began to show itself in the east and Dumpster turned toward the west, toward the Badger river, scant yards on the other side of a sandy, grapevine-strewn peninsula. He saw the sun brighten the dawn on the village of Plum across the river and watched its light climb down the three church steeples Uptop. He was in a mood for reflection. He rubbed a hand over his crew-cut hair and leaned his broad back against the motor. The sight of the three churches always put a question in Dumpster's head. Something about them just don't make sense, he thought. What do their differences add to what the Bible and Ben Franklin had to say?

Dumpster remembered the last time he had been Uptop, the time the priest, Jack Tyrrell, called and asked could he rid the rectory of a family of raccoons that had taken a fancy to the soffit on the garage. Dumpster had obliged and got a prompt note of thanks. He recalled how he had brought the young priest, Chicago born and raised, out on the river to fish. Jack had never fished. In the boat he'd been like that china-closet bull, tangling his feet in the anchor line, banging the anchor and making enough noise to reach a walleye clear up in Canada. Dumpster laughed out loud at the memory of how he had gingerly snaked a hooked plug from Jack's rear end after a too enthusiastic cast. Jack had spent half that trip sorting tangled lines from his reel.

"Don't give up on me, Dumpster," Jack had said, picking away at the bird nest in his reel, "I'll get the hang of it yet."

And Jack had got the hang of it. Dumpster felt a tinge of pride rise up at the part he played. Too bad the priest was so busy he didn't get to spend much time up front in this boat, a disappointment now to Dumpster. The word on Main Street had it that Jack was also in a tangle with his bishop, which didn't make sense. Seems that church could use a slew of Jacks.

Dumpster watched the sunlight work its way down the hill. Near the bottom, but still on a downslope, the bigger houses of the village were strung like lights facing the river. Doc Robyn and her husband, Jim, had their home there. Dumpster saw the white of its columns come alive in the sun. Now, there's a no-nonsense young woman, he thought. Ben Franklin said, *Beware the young doctor and the old barber.* Dumpster reckoned this was one of the few times Ben had it wrong. This young doctor was good.

When the sun reached the river and highlighted its mottled whirlpools and wind-swept ruffles, Dumpster looked across at his own home, nestled just south of the village where the railroad tracks turned away from the river and gave room for homes that set close to the banks. How many years now was it that he had left the homeplace? Twenty? He could see the open door of his boathouse. Becky had lived in that home for nearly five years with him before the wander-lust took control.

When the sun struck Dumpster's back he decided to soak in it for awhile. His mind wandered upstream to his home place. Wouldn't Uncle Hiram and Aunt Rachel get a kick out of a morning like this. Dumpster was a baby when his father had been killed over in Korea. He couldn't remember his mother. Bereaved, she simply wandered off somewhere. She never came back. Hiram and Rachel became mother and father to the sprouting Dumpster. Images of the rotund Rachel and the tall, thin, scraggly-bearded Hiram flowed at slough speed in Dumpster. Rachel was all warm hugs, cakes and kitchen. Hiram was wit and earth-drawn wisdom.

"You just live by the Bible and by Benjamin Franklin, young feller," Hiram had advised, his lanky arm around

Dumpster's shoulder, "and you ain't gonna stray too far from the right track." Dumpster picked up the habit himself, just from the exposure. *Men and melons are hard to know,* Benjamin said. Hiram agreed but kept on trying. So did Dumpster. You just don't give up on people.

Images of Rachel and Hiram in their final years filled Dumpster with a nostalgic sadness. Rachel's body and mind withered in tandem. Hiram would bend over her bed each morning desperate for a sign of recognition. Rachel's rare "Oh-h-h Hiram" lit his entire day. Rachel's passing sparked Hiram's own rapid decline and death.

If it hadn't been for Becky, Dumpster thought, I'd just as soon gone myself. Becky, Becky. His eyes were on the dark slough waters as pictures of Becky floated to the surface; the dark-haired, snub-nosed tiny mite she was in the first grade; the thin, two-inch taller than him Becky in the eighth; the cute round-faced Becky whose height and size he had long dwarfed by their senior year; the lush-lipped Becky who gave him his first kiss.

Dumpster had inherited the farm from Hiram about the time he graduated from high school. He didn't much take to the life of a farmer. He sold the cattle but continued to cash crop the place while he studied police science at the technical school over at Stockford. Dumpster studied, dated Becky and, in the summer time, worked the fields. Their marriage when Dumpster graduated and got the constable job in Plum was just another seamless move in their relationship. As it surfaced, he held onto the picture of her, veiled in white, on their wedding day, a rounder, softer Becky. They had married at twenty. They bought a home in Plum and kept the farm. Dumpster had time to work it in his off-hours.

Becky got a job as a waitress at the *Plum Turnover*. She liked meeting new people, especially folks from other places. She read a lot, novels and travel magazines. She began to talk about travel frequently, those exotic places out there, the

"French Quarter in New Orleans, Fisherman's Wharf at San Francisco, New York's Time Square, the Eiffel Tower in Paris."

Four years into their marriage, Becky came into the house one day with the mail.

"A letter from my cousin in Savannah," she shouted to Dumpster. She ripped it open. "Ruthie wants me to come there for a visit, Dumpster," she said as he joined her in the kitchen.

"You should go, Becky," he responded. He didn't have the desire, but wanted her to go. She went, and came home with an appetite whetted instead of satiated.

Less than a month after her return from Georgia, she again came in with the mail and tore open a letter. Dumpster was sitting at the kitchen table oiling a fishing reel.

"I won it!" she screamed. "I won it!" She waved a sheaf of papers at him.

"Won what?" Dumpster asked.

"I won us a trip to New York. You remember that contest sponsored by the FoodMart over in Stockford? Oh, look at these. I also won us theater tickets to shows on Broadway. Can you believe it?" She held up the tickets. Dumpster went to New York with Becky, but came home with the clear understanding that she would do her traveling without him in the future. He just didn't cotton to it. She went alone to San Diego and with a local group to London. Looking back, Dumpster thought, that idea of travel became a constant itch somewhere inside her.

The memory of that fateful day forced itself on Dumpster. Becky was arranging a vase of lilac cuttings at a kitchen counter. Dumpster was at the table.

Becky turned to him, her face tearing. "I can't live in Plum any longer, honey. There's too big a world out there. I love you, and I'm not going to somebody else. I just need to go. I just need to go...places."

He could still feel their parting hug when he put her on the bus with a caring pat to her plump behind. He sold the farm after she left and used the money to keep her going. The money was about gone when she wrote telling him she had this terrific job that kept her traveling, and she wouldn't be needing any more money. She would keep in touch. And she did. He would get cards and letters, not often, but always from some far away place he didn't know about.

Dumpster reached for his billfold and extracted the picture of Becky he had taken on their honeymoon in Yellowstone Park. There she stood in front of Old Faithful. In some ways it's easier now, he thought. There's relief in not having to watch her everyday discontent. She'll come back some day, won't she? She's the prodigal spouse. There was just something in her system that needs emptying. And I'll be waiting. In the meantime there's all the people in Plum. A bear of a man, Dumpster still rubbed moisture from his eyes onto his sleeve. He spoke a prayer out loud. "Thanks for the fish. Thanks for a sunny day. Keep Becky safe. Amen."

The jangle of his cell phone broke the spell of memories. He answered and listened for a moment. His face sobered. "I'll be there in ten minutes, Doc."

He quickly hauled in the trolling bucket and the anchor, and pulled the motor alive. As the boat rounded the entrance to the slough and headed across the river, his eyes searched the business district. Temple Swift was raising the American flag on top of the tallest building in Plum, three stories high. It housed the office and printing facilities of the *Plum Predicate.* Swift lived on the third floor. He was owner, editor and chief reporter.

The news hasn't reached Temple yet, Dumpster thought. Pulling close to the Plum shore he raced south toward his home. Beth Halkerston, the pharmacist, was sitting on a riverside bench having her coffee and breakfast. She waved and he returned it. Bethy hasn't heard yet either.

***

A few neighbors stood outside the house when Dumpster pulled up to the Chase home.

He nodded to them as he walked to the door. Doc Robyn was waiting inside.

"He's dead, Dumpster," she said. " I've called the coroner and the sheriff's office. They should be here before long. There's nothing more I can do. The news is out and will be all over town in minutes." There were tears in her eyes. "I can't help wondering, did we fail John in some way? Could we have prevented this?"

When Robyn left, Dumpster examined the living room. It was easy enough to reconstruct the scene and John Plum Chase's last moments. He spied the scribbled note and picked it up."

"I'm too lonely here," it read simply. "I go to where the smiles are."

CHAPTER SEVEN

Maggie was off early this morning as usual to the University. Felicity made an early morning trip to the grocery store for some supplies. When I joined her for breakfast on her return, she said that the store was abuzz with talk of a local suicide.

"He must have been much loved," she said. "The people all seem dejected, despondent."

"Did you find out anything about the man?" I asked.

"A little. He was elderly. Eighty, someone said. A fourth generation member of the community. Evidently, he was also something of a philanthropist. His name was John Plum Chase. There's some connection between the name of the village and his middle name. That's about all I got."

I confess that the import of Felicity's news did not strike me with any particular force. We included John Plum Chase in our prayer before breakfast and turned to other topics. It was not until this afternoon that I began to appreciate the magnitude of this man's death.

Within an hour of my return home last week after my unsuccessful attempt at surfing, I received a visit from Temple Swift. His wide face and graying forelock rested on a casually-dressed trim body. He wore a look more serious than my own, I think, but was himself a most pleasant man. He introduced himself as the editor of the local weekly, the *Plum Predicate*, and presented me with a copy of the current issue which I have since read cover to cover. I am much impressed by the depth and logic of its editorial content.

Temple invited me to join a group of local clergy who meet at a weekly luncheon. He had formed the group originally to collect material for his paper. I was delighted at the invitation, but accepted with some apprehension. The group met this noon at the *Plum Turnover*, Shelly Burg's place, a clean, bright cafe located at the foot of the hill where our street intersects Main Street. I passed it on my rush to the river. Today I took a more controlled pace to the cafe.

There were six of us seated at a round table in a windowed corner of the cafe. My view went half to the tables and half to the hill and the three churches Uptop. In age I was the senior, perhaps along with Grace Jensen. Grace, a slim and attractive lady with graying dark hair, is the soft-spoken pastor of Gethsemane Evangelical Lutheran Church Uptop. Paul Staunton, about mid-fifties, a youthful face shaded under salt and pepper hair, is the pastor of the Pilgrim United Church of Christ. Erudition streams through his eyes and tongue. I'd already met Jack Tyrrell. He has been pastor of St. Anne's here for four years. Jack eyed me warily at first, evidently having failed to connect with my identity after Mass on Sunday. But he seemed to relax as the conversation progressed. My newly found friend, Dumpster Heap, completed our half dozen.

The restaurant was packed. Shelly and her staff were constantly adding folding chairs to already full tables. The name Chase kept reoccurring in snippets of conversation that floated above the crowd. It was clear that these men and women were deeply affected by Chase's death and had gathered in such numbers from an inner need. Then a parade began. People got up from their tables and came to ours. They expressed their need to examine the whys of it all. The theme of guilt and gloom repeated itself over and over. "What did we do wrong? How could this happen in Plum? How can a person become so lonely here that he or she would take their own life? How do we make sure this doesn't happen again?" They sensed a flaw in this, their society, and wanted it fixed.

Their underlying request was directed at the pastors. You take charge of this. You find out why this happened. You tell us what we must do to prevent any such thing in the future.

Eventually the parade ceased and the crowd began to thin. I saw Shelly Burg, Maggie's good friend, wind her way from table to table greeting customers, checking their satisfaction, and joining their grief. The lights created flashes on her strawberry blond hair, punctuating her movements. As she approached our table I could see a seriousness in her eyes.

"You holy folks got all the world's problems solved yet?" she asked.

"All but one," Paul Staunton countered.

"What's that?" Shelly asked.

"It's the blueberry pie. How do we get you to make bigger slices?"

Mischief replaced the serious look for a moment. "Paul, you can always buy a second piece." She looked around the table, greeted each of us by name, and asked, "Any more problems? If not, I've got one for you."

"Our turn is it?" Jack asked. "Not too difficult now."

She pointed Uptop. "There's the problem in this town. Uptop. Three churches up there. Down here we're together. We work together. We play together. We try to help each other when we see a need. Uptop we're divided, separated. What's the important thing in being Christian anyway? Doesn't it mean being together? No wonder a man like John Plum Chase could get lost in the cracks. The divisions up there make room for the cracks. Don't you think you all ought to do something about that?" She moved on to the next table, a smile and a look of mischief replacing her serious demeanor.

Shelly's challenge brought a measured sobriety to the group.

After a pause, Temple asked quietly, "Do you want to tackle that one?"

We looked at each other. Grace finally broke the silence.

"I need to think about this. I've just never thought about it other than poetically, like each of us having a piece of the truth, a piece of the puzzle. The thought of putting the puzzle together...well, I don't know..."

"We've got a building Uptop," Paul said. "But I already spend most of my time down below with the people. I've got some parishioners who think I should be spending all my time Uptop."

Jack, eyes on me, asked. "Isn't it a problem for church leaders?"

"Church leaders? What are you? Spare ribs?" Temple asked.

Jack was still looking at me, his question meant for me.

"We've been fragmenting for centuries," I said. "Once it began, the fragmentation seemed to accelerate. We should remember this about church leaders. They're human. They have a vested interest in their own turfs. How fast do you think they're moving on Shelly's challenge?"

I saw surprise register in Jack's eyes, and I could see that Temple was relishing this topic.

"Suppose we got together in one church, wouldn't that be just another fragmentation, just one more new denomination?" Grace asked.

"Let's put this on our agenda," Jack said.

"I'm for that," Grace said. "I need time to think."

"I'm in," Paul said. "This should be interesting."

"I think Shelly's put her finger right where the sore is," Dumpster said.

As for myself, I'm going to enjoy this as much as any of you, I thought. What's more, I'm floating again, this time in the social current of Plum.

***

My new phone system has once again opened up the world to my voice. I can call and receive calls on my computer. No hands, one finger. No one has to hold a phone to my ear. I'm elated.

The honor of my first incoming call goes to Stan (Starchy) McIntyre. We were classmates in the seminary. Starchy is an addict of law and order. He knows and lives by every minute rule and ritual in the books. That knowledge and habit brought him to the episcopacy. He is now the bishop of this diocese, and Jack Tyrrell is one of his priests. As we talked I had a clear vision of Starchy aligning and realigning a stapler on his desk in perfect symmetry with the straight line of his breviary. His deep, resonant voice brought back the memory of a talk where he expounded on how All-might-y Gawd had taken up residence in the canons and rituals of the Church.

"I would have called earlier, Fred," he said today, "but you know how demanding this job is."

"Good to hear from you, Starchy." I know only too well how demanding. Starchy is an industrious man. However, I'm not sure at what that industry is pointed. For many of our peers, much of their energy goes to their careers, making contacts, writing letters of condolence or congratulations to clerics of higher status, or whatever might move their careers to the next higher level. They move in circles where ambition is considered the fifth cardinal virtue, along with prudence, justice, fortitude and temperance. After all, the thinking goes, is ambition wrong if it's in the service of God?

"I'm sorry to hear about your affliction. My prayers."

"Thanks."

"I understand that you still get around, though. How's that going?"

"Come out here sometime. I'll let you drive Rover, my new trusty steed."

"I'll do that. In the meantime I have a favor to ask."

"Shoot."

"Have you met the pastor in Plum, Jack Tyrrell?"

"Yes. I was at a luncheon with him and several other local notables just this week. I think I'm going to like him."

"Well, I'm hearing that he's on the wild side when it comes to the rules. Likes to hike outside the fence, so to speak. If you see anything egregious I'd like to know about it."

"Starchy, you're going to get complaints on anyone who's trying to do their job. I'd worry about the ones you don't get gripes about."

"Wel-l-l, we have to have rules, Fred. You know that."

"We've got a lot of them, Starchy. How many do we need?"

"Har, har, har. When did you get to be such a clown, Fred? Sure we need them. How else do we control things?"

"Control people, you mean?"

"You know what I mean, Fred. You're a Roman guy. Anyway, keep an eye on Tyrrell for me. I don't like to wait too long before I clobber the rule breakers. It's the only way to keep order."

"If Jack kills someone, you'll be the first to know, Starchy."

"Har, har, har. Take care, Fred. When my schedule lets me, I'll come over and try out your Rover."

I wonder if Starchy's schedule will let that happen. I'm liking Jack more already. He'll challenge authority to look at itself. He tested me.

JOURNAL - June 23

Starchy's call led me to reflect on power. I know something about it. I have used power in my ministry. But what sticks with me is the many times that I misused it. I see now that power and its use belong in the context of love of neighbor. It is a component of that love. It is part of the gift of self, a bestowal of trust on the other. The appropriate analogy for power in a Christian context is the love between husband and wife, or between friends. The loving person takes on vulnerability by this transfer of power to the spouse or friend, the power to exact a response to needs, but also the power to inflict hurt. I cannot love my neighbor without bestowing trust. I may be bruised in return, but I must offer it. How can I say I accept you, but refuse to empower you with trust?

Rejection then becomes almost a statistical necessity in the life of a Christian. It's going to happen. It happened to the One who showed us this Way. When it happens we withdraw just out of range and stand open for another try. And we continue to meet the needs that we can.

What I failed to realize in my own ministry, and what my fellow bishops fail to realize, is that the use of power in a Christian context is always an exchange, a mutual empowerment of the other. We bishops have taken on ourselves power, not in an exchange, but as overlords, contrary to the explicit mandate given us: "You know how those who exercise authority among the Gentiles lord it over them; their great ones make their importance felt. It cannot be like that with you. Anyone among you who aspires to greatness must serve the rest, and whoever wants to rank first among you must serve the needs of all." (Mt. 20:25ff)

Never, since we bishops adopted our monarchical lifestyle centuries ago, have we given trust to the hearts and minds of the laity. We speak officially of a "Sense of the Faithful," but at best only pretend to give it serious hearing. In not trusting them, neither do we trust the Spirit of God Who speaks to us through them. Examples like birth control, mandatory celibacy and women's ordination come to mind, where the vast majority of laity differ from their bishops. We never carry their voices to the Vatican with insistence. What does that say about our courage? About our credibility when we posture as moral leaders? About our own ability to love our neighbor?

When it comes to loving others, I have a personal history of going the wrong power route. And now, I feel so inadequate for the real task. God, help me to learn.

CHAPTER EIGHT

Paul Staunton stood on the Plum depot's red brick platform waiting for the 7:36 a.m. commuter to Chicago's Union Station. His gaze rose to his own Pilgrim Church Uptop and the classic lines of its steeple, whitening in the sun. Seventeen years as pastor, he mused. Seventeen good years despite the independent thinking and sometimes contentious members. Thank God, he thought, for both qualities.

He watched the chairperson of his Board of Trustees, Marvin Principle, enter the Village Hall, Plum's Administrative Center, across the street. The Center was housed in a former five-and-dime store. Take Marvin, Paul thought, a good, solid member. Marvin lives on personal responsibility and self-reliance, and believes firmly that his way is God's way. He has no time for the shiftless as he calls the poor. They are destitute by their own design, and deservedly. Yet I know him to be personally generous, even as he keeps a thrifty watch on the church's expenditures. When listening to a sermon, like so many people he will hear only what vindicates his own perspective of things -- the world according to Marvin. And he is quick to pass judgment on anyone who lives and thinks differently.

Another parishioner, Hannah Stuart, called a "good morning, Paul" from her car as she rode to work. Paul waved back, thinking there goes the other side of my congregation. Hannah is heart, smart heart. She will suffer with anyone who suffers, no matter what the malady. Still, she's tough. She holds her own with Marvin.

The train switched tracks to pull into the station. Plum was the commuter's end-of-line. Paul went aboard and took a seat on the village side of the car. As the train began to roll he saw Shelly Burg's car pull up to the IGA store. Restaurant probably needs eggs or bacon, he thought. Now, how would a Marvin Principle react to Shelly's challenge? Or a Hannah Stuart? He felt he knew what Hannah's response would be. But Marvin? And me, how should I react to the challenge? I preach inclusion, but I've never thought about it outside the box of my own congregation. Can I think outside that box? If the message of the good Samaritan is that we don't *have* neighbors, but *make* ourselves a neighbor, can I refuse to reach out? He turned his thoughts to his day ahead at the homeless shelter.

***

Marvin Principle stared at the green marble walls of the men's room stall. Seated ramrod straight on a throne in the Village Hall, he countered the irritation of having seen Paul Staunton on the commuter platform. Off to the city, he thought, to coddle homeless bums. Waste of time. Bums are bums. They could make it if they had any spunk. I did, by God. I started with zilch. Now I own a bank.

Every morning in that same stall Marvin reviewed the habits that governed his life. The first was thrift. It's at least an eight to twelve gallon savings on water by using this public toilet, he thought. In a year's time that's a tidy savings. Cutting my floss at exactly thirteen inches yields more savings. The list went on until Marvin left the building and emerged into the summer light. His irritation returned as he watched Staunton get on the train. That man has made a lot of changes in our church since he came on board, and not for the better in my opinion. A man of lists, Marvin began to run down the slate of irritations that Paul Staunton had inserted into his orderly life. He says that not everything in the Bible happened the way it says they did. Imagine! My God, if you can't take the Bible for what it says, what good is it? He didn't take me in on that one. Then he gets the members to agree that anyone, I mean anyone, even a drunken bum is welcome to partake at the communion service. Good Lord, would you want a dirty, drunken bum at your table? I'll accept bums when they get a job.

And last month, just last month, Staunton suggests to the cabinet the idea that we become what he calls an open and affirming church. What he means is, open and welcoming to homosexuals, gays and lesbians. You can't exclude anybody, he says. Well, I don't buy that. He wouldn't last long running my loan department, I can tell you that. Thank God we don't have any more of those homosexual types here in Plum. I'll accept homosexuals when hell freezes over. Just one more crazy idea out of Staunton and I'm going after his hide.

Marvin's daughter, Mary, waved from her bicycle as she rode by with her friend, Danielle. He waved back. Two peas in a pod, he thought. Summer soccer today. She's as good as the son I always wanted. Marvin's life centered on three things: Mary, his only child, and only family since his wife, Selma, had passed on two years back; the bank; and Pilgrim Church. Now, thanks to Paul Staunton, only the church seemed in danger of escaping Marvin's idea of how it ought to be run. And he felt his responsibility.

***

At worship service the following Sunday, Paul Staunton stood in the center aisle of Pilgrim church to deliver his message.

"My dear friends. We have all lost a friend in John Plum Chase. Even though John was not a member of our congregation, I will speak to his passing and to its significance this morning. To begin, I offer you a picture of Jesus that is not found explicitly in the Gospels, that it gives us a true and closer understanding of who He was and what His message was.

"As he approached the entrance to a small village one day, he saw an old woman sitting at the side of the road, begging. He stopped in front of her and said, 'Good morning.'

"Shocked, she looked down at the ground and was speechless. She was a woman, and men did not talk to strange women, unless it was to give an order, a demand that she *do* something for him. So she mumbled a polite greeting, but continued to stare at the ground, for women did not look strange men in the eye.

"Then the man said to her, 'I would like to stay at your home today. Would you share your lunch with me?' Now she was flabbergasted. She had no idea how to respond. She stuttered and stammered. 'I...I...I have very little to eat,' she said, 'and my house is a mess.' 'Don't worry. I will share what you have,' he said, and he reached down to take her arm and help her to her feet.

"The woman's hut was on the outskirts of the village, together with those of people who were considered *unclean* by the more respectable villagers. While she seemed ashamed of her place, he seemed not to notice its crudeness and utter lack of amenities. She brought each of them a piece of bread and a cup of water. They sat on crude chairs at a rough table. After a minute or two of silence, the man pointed. 'Do you see that cockroach?' They watched it scurry across the dirt floor. 'Isn't it beautiful?' he asked. 'Look how gracefully it moves.' She laughed at the strangeness of his remark. Their eyes met and they laughed together. She realized she had not laughed in a long time.

"Hearing the laughter, a neighbor woman poked her head in the door to see what the laughter was all about. The two women had never become friends, though they lived close together. The old woman was poor and of a lower class than her neighbor, who was from a higher status family, but had sores on her face and arms, and for that reason was unclean and not allowed in the village. The old woman bristled at the intrusion, but the man invited the neighbor in. Soon the three were talking amiably and laughing together. Others heard them and joined them. Some went to get food and wine, and soon they were all laughing with this entertaining man at the center of the party.

"At a pause in the conversation, the man asked quietly, 'Do you feel what is happening here? Do you sense the power we have when we include everyone in our group who wants to be in? We have the power to heal one another's pain.'"

Paul paused for a moment to let the picture sink into the minds of his congregation.

"You know," he continued:

"Here at Pilgrim Church we look upon ourselves as an open and affirming community, an inclusive community. We welcome everyone who wants to be with us in our church. It is a wonderful quality of our congregation. But, can we be more? Is it enough to sit in isolation and include everyone who wants to be with us in this particular church? This church sits adjacent to Lutheran and Roman Catholic churches. Their members are our brothers and sisters. Does our willingness to include others carry with it a willingness to be included *by* others? Did our separateness leave open a space for John Plum Chase to hide his desperate loneliness? Should we be looking for ways to move closer to them and to others? I ask each of you to ponder this and give me your thoughts."

As Paul greeted members as they left the Church, Marvin Principle, accompanied by his daughter Mary, stopped in front of him. Marvin's voice reflected the stiffness of his body. "Nothing for me to think about, Paul. They're there. We're here. Leave it that way. We've gone too damn far as it is."

***

You knew Marvin Principle's home by the twin stone turrets that sat astride its front corners. The house stood on the same tier as the old Kelly place, Dr. Horsager's and other old majestic homes. Only Marvin's house was new, built on the site of a razed gothic. As large and tall as the others, it was a fortress in comparison, enclosed in Indiana limestone and architecturally reminiscent of early twentieth century banks. Elongated bay windows fronted the side toward the town and river.

Marvin sat in the stuffed puffs of a leather chair near the window of his den and worked his way through the week's stack of Wall Street Journals, his regular Sunday enjoyment. He circled items of interest with a red, felt-tip pen for cutting and saving. The den was appointed with a large, polished maple desk, a leather swivel chair, two of the stuffed variety occupied by Marvin, maple bookcases and two maple file cabinets. The surround of bookcases was neatly stacked with books, the titles of which covered the fields of economics, banking and investments. A Bible rested on the small table next to Marvin's chair.

"Come and get it, Dad," Mary called from the dining room where she and her friend, Danielle, stood waiting. The room was festooned with multicolored streamers and balloons. As Marvin entered the room the girls began a snappy "Happy Birthday to You," and followed it with an "How O-o-old are You" to the same tune.

Marvin smiled and his posture relaxed perceptibly. It's good, he thought. If Selma were here now, it'd be as good as it gets. He sat as the girls held his chair and then led them in saying grace.

After Mary ended the prayer with "And God bless my Dad on his birthday," she took the lid from a large earthenware platter set in front of Marvin. A pot roast was centered there surrounded by mounds of carrots, potatoes, mushrooms, cabbage and parsnips.

"My favorite," he exclaimed. "You girls sure know where my heart is." He looked from one to the other with obvious pleasure; to Mary, his lovely, raven-haired daughter and to Danielle, pretty also with her pixie-styled blond hair. Like sisters, he thought. He picked up the carving knife, turned the platter enough to let him cut against the meat's grain, and carved with precision. "Your plates, please," he instructed.

The girls handed him their plates in turn and he filled them, then his own. Tasting the meat he uttered a contented "mmmmmm," and ate for a time in silence. Then, "So, what've you girls been up to, besides preparing this feast?" he asked.

"We were playing soccer," Mary replied.

"We're determined to make the team at Midwestern this fall," Danni added.

"As freshmen? Wow! That would be something," Marvin said. "Good luck. You know, I think you two just might do it."

At meal's end, the girls cleared the dishes and emerged from the kitchen with a candle-lighted chocolate cake.

"Any more candles on that and we'd need the fire department on standby," Marvin said, and then blew.

Mary laid two colorful, wrapped presents on the table near her Dad's plate. He opened them between bites, a hand-held, print-out calculator and a box of red felt-tip pens.

"Just what I need," Marvin said. "Thank you both." He finished his cake. "What's on your agenda tonight?" he asked.

"We'll clean up in the kitchen," Mary replied, " and then, if its okay, I'll spend the night at Danni's. We've got so much planning to do for college."

"You have a good time," he said.

CHAPTER NINE

Beth Halkerston took the last bite of her carrot muffin and stuffed a napkin into an empty coffee mug. She took a final glance at the morning sun as it rose over the bottom lands across the river, then watched a tiny eddy slowly swirl its way upstream from a wing dam and dissolved itself into the cement embankment. She sounded a contented sigh and said a prayer of thanks to the God of dawn's glory. She stood up from the stone bench, turned and walked across the railroad tracks, her eyes scanning the three-block length of small-town-America store fronts across the street.

At the door of the Plum Drug Store she pulled a leather string necklace over her head and turned its sole ornament, a long bulky key, in the keyhole. Inside the store, Beth walked to the utility room in the back and filled a bucket with warm water, splashed ammonia into it, grabbed the long handled brush and squeegee and returned to the outside storefront. In minutes the huge plate-glass front shone clean in the early morning light. She inspected the appearance of the upper story; the white trim, the geranium-filled flower boxes of its two windows, and the false gable that soared in red brick splendor above the roof. Old things and old ways brought her inner warmth. She gave a gentle pat to the brickwork.

Back inside, Beth sprinkled a handful of oiled sweeping compound onto the plank floor and set her petite body on the push side of the broom, enjoying the old fashioned sweep in each of the three aisles. On both of the long walls display cases rose to a height of seven feet. Between the aisles two elongated and terraced islands rose to a height just below Beth's eyeline. She hummed an octave-high *Old Man River* as her eyes moved back and forth from the floor to the display islands.

At the back of the store three stacks of old library shelves intruded eight feet into the room. These were the shelves on which she had arranged her prescription drugs. A waist-high counter carried an antique bronze cash register, and guarded the drug area against unlicensed intrusion. Beth was busy checking her inventory on these shelves when she heard the morning freight train come to a halt on the track across the street, its line of cars braying harsh metallic words against the brakeman. Normally the mournful whistle and the train's rumble along the riverbank lay just beyond her awareness. The Coach Factory must have another car ready for delivery, she thought, and then forgot the train as she jotted down items to order.

Beth went forward to the vitamin display to return misplaced containers to their proper place. Some customers weren't choosy where they put an item if they picked it up by mistake. She heard the tinkle of its bell as the shop door opened. Thinking it signaled the newspaper delivery she voiced a "Morning Harry," over her shoulder. A mumbled reply and the slam of the door answered her. She kept at her task. A few moments later she was startled by an arm that circled her waist, and another that brought a shard of glass over head and pressed its jagged edge to her neck. Beth froze. Her heart raced and pounded in her chest.

"Drugs," a man's voice croaked as he pulled her to the rear of the store and behind the cash register.

Beth pointed to the middle shelf in the drug section.

The man pulled her backwards to the shelf and turned her to it, locking her legs between his own. He kept the shard's pressure on her neck.

"What drug?" she asked.

"MS Contin."

She looked down at his feet. He wore only socks, grayed white, a large toe protruding through one of them. She pointed upwards again toward the upper shelf, unable to reach higher because of his grip. She felt a slight release of his hold, raised her right foot and slammed her hard rubber heel into his instep. The man cursed through a groan and loosed one arm. She dropped her body, let her knees give, and fell through his grip. On the floor she crawled a few feet, stood and raced away.

The man clumsily limped a few steps, but came after her.

She ran toward the door, clearing a shelf of vitamin bottles as she passed by. As she reached the door she heard him fall. Her foot caught one of the man's shoes and kicked it through the open door as she ran outside and up the middle of the street.

"Bethy, what's the matter?" Dumpster Heap's bass voice met her as she came even with the bank. Heap was at the bank's door, checking its lock.

Beth stopped running, her heart a rapid flutter. Unable to speak, she pointed back down the street.

Dumpster stepped out of the recessed doorway.

The man chasing Beth also stopped on hearing Dumpster's voice. At the sight of the constable he turned and started to run. He soon slowed, chest heaving, to a trot.

Heap wrapped a huge arm around the man's sallow neck, and quickly snapped handcuffs on his wrists.

Beth walked to a bench in front of the bank, sat and watched as Dumpster led her shoeless assailant to the bench anchored in front of the drug store. She took deep breaths and gradually her pounding heart slowed. She watched Heap retrieve the shoe she had kicked from the store, kneel and put it on the man's foot. As Dumpster worked the laces, she marveled at his gentle kindness. If I were Dumpster's size, I'd beat the guy bloody, she thought.

Dumpster found the man's second shoe and was leading him by the elbow toward her. Beth stood.

Heap gently pushed the man onto the bench. "You just sit there and behave, sir," he instructed. "I don't like my exercise this early in the mornin'."

Beth felt her heart begin to race again. "I don't know where he came from" she said, a breath between each sentence. "Maybe the train. I didn't hear him. He grabbed me from behind. Held some broken glass against my neck."

"Take your time now, Bethy," Dumpster said reasssuringly. "We got all the time in the world. This gentleman won't mind. Will you, sir?"

The man sat, his head turned downward. His pallid complexion showed on a wrinkled neck. He said nothing.

"He wanted drugs, the easy living kind." She felt her neck. A dab of blood moistened her fingers. "Looks like he nicked me a little."

Dumpster bent to look at her neck. "Just a nick is right, Bethy. A wash cloth will take care of it." He turned to the man and read him his rights. "Is that what happened, sir?"

No response.

"Well, sir, you have plumb spoiled my day. There's a school of blue gills just waitin' for me out there." He pointed to the river. "Now I've got to take you over to the county seat and have you registered for new quarters. So I'd take it kindly if you'd behave, as I'm not presently in the mood for any tomfoolery. What's your name?"

No response. The man sat, motionless.

A car pulled up to the curb. The window rolled down and Robyn Horsager called out, "Is there a problem here?"

"Hi, Doc. You take Bethy here to the cafe," Dumpster replied, bending to the window. "She can use a bit of calmin' down. She'll tell you about it. Bethy, you go with Doc Robyn now." He pulled a ring of keys from his belt. "I'll lock the pharmacy on my way by. Then I'll see to our friend here. After that I'll come by with a statement for you to sign."

"It's a mess in there," Beth replied.

"You can clean up the mess later," Dumpster said calmly, and opened the car door.

Robyn and Beth took a booth in the Plum Turnover. Robyn ordered tea for Beth, and coffee for herself.

Beth began to shake again and had trouble with her cup.

Robyn reached in her handbag, brought out a bottle and dispensed a capsule to Beth.

"Take this," she instructed, and helped Beth hold her glass of water steady. "You'll be fine in a few minutes. Good. Now try a few sips of this tea." Again she helped steady the cup. "Isn't that Dumpster something else?"

"He's great," Beth replied. "I was never so happy to see someone in my life."

"Did you ever hear how he got the name, Dumpster?"

"No."

"He was a local football hero. Played on the right side of the line. Folks said he *was* the right side of the line. Stood there like a dumpster and nobody got by him. The team started calling him Dumpster. And it took. Soon the cheerleaders and crowds were yelling, Dumpster! Dumpster! Dumpster! Later when he went to the Technical College he introdued himself as Dumpster Heap. Asked why, he said it was a step up from Hezekiah. No question, though, he was proud of the name and how he got it."

"How did he get to be constable here?" Beth asked.

"I was just a teenager at the time. The former peace officer retired at the same time Dumpster finished his associate degree in Police Science. Dumpster was a shoo-in, local legend and all that. I guess Dumpster liked the sound of constable better than peace officer. Anyway, the council obliged him. He's been Constable Dumpster Heap ever since." Robyn studied her former college roommate. "You ready to talk about it?"

Beth took a deep breath. "At first I thought it was Ed...."

***

Ferocious Creek came out of the north and turned east as it butted against the hill that carried Uptop. It flowed along a shallow ravine at the back edge of the Halkerston yard and wound toward Main Street where, just after skirting the Predicate building, it went beneath the street's bridge and a railroad trestle before blending into the river.

Village children were quick to take possession of its mysteries, though most left it quickly for the greater excitement of sport fields and the river itself. Not so Beth Halkerston's daughter, Annie. At age six she was princess of this realm.

Whoever named Ferocious Creek did so with an evident sense of humor. At an average depth of three inches, and a few treacherous holes as deep as six inches, it held all the danger of pablum. Its source was a spring several miles north which guaranteed a steady flow of water. Rain, even downpours, seldom effected an increase in depth of more than an inch. Parents had made it open territory for any child over five. Despite the creek's benign character, Temple Swift felt a kind of responsibility for the safety of the children and kept sporadic watch over the area from his office window at the Predicate. His surveillance had yet to call for more than a rare application of a band-aid.

Temple sat penning his weekly editorial. From time to time he looked up at a portrait on his desk. His wife, Maureen, their five year old daughter, Megan, and he himself beamed wide smiles at the viewer. He became captivated by the smiles, mostly his own. Where did that go, he wondered? The photo was fifteen years old, taken a week before Maureen and Megan were both killed, crushed in a tangle of automobile when a drunken tourist hit them with his pickup. Had he really smiled like that since? If he had, was it with that same inner feeling, or was it only a social cosmetic? I'm too damn serious. I need some sort of remedy, he thought. What ingredients should go into Temple Swift's Elixir of Ready Joy?

Glancing out his window he saw the familiar form of Annie Halkerston. She waded the creek, a salad-plate size net in her hand. Her face flushed with the moment's joy. He stood and walked out a side door. "Hi, Annie. What are you looking for today?" he asked, approaching the creek.

Annie looked up. "Hi, Mr. Swift. I'm lookin' for a frog."

Temple squatted on the bank. "That's a fine looking net you've got there."

"My Dad made it for me."

"You sure look happy today, Annie. Are you happy all the time?"

Annie wiped her nose with the back of her hand. "Mostly, I guess. Except sometimes when my brothers fight with me. But I like to fight too. It's fun to be mad sometimes. How come you don't smile so much, Mr. Swift?"

"I guess I forgot how. How come you smile all the time?"

"It's funner than bein' sad."

"I think you're on to something there, Annie."

"Bet I can teach you."

"Teach me what?"

"How to be funner."

"Well now, that would be worth a lot, maybe even a double decker ice cream cone over at the Turnover."

"First you gotta take off your shoes and roll up your pants."

Temple bent to comply. "Okay, now what?"

"We skip."

"We skip?"

"Sure. Follow me." She took off skipping upstream, head and shoulders swaying with each skip, kicking the water forward.

Temple followed and soon caught the rhythm. He kicked the water high and soaked his trousers. By the time they skipped the distance to Annie's backyard and back, Temple felt a buoyancy rise in him, and was outright pooped. He bent over to catch his breath, but couldn't help laughing.

"See, Mr. Swift, you can't be sad when you're skippin'."

You're right again, Annie, and you're a good teacher. Let's go get that ice cream."

Cone in hand, Temple said, "I can't skip all the time, Annie. What do I do then?"

Annie swiped her tongue up the sides of her ice cream. "You do fun stuff, Mr. Swift."

"Will you come back and show me fun stuff?"

"Sure I will."

Back in his office, Temple skipped again, wall to wall. Forget the elixir, he thought. The wisdom of a child! Why don't we adults listen to them more? He heard the bell clang as someone entered. He left his office to find Dumpster waiting at the counter.

***

Beth looked up at the jangle of the door bell to see Temple Swift stride in.

"Aha, Beth," he declared. "Our stalwart constable has just related to me your early morning encounter with a scoundrel. I have come to ascertain the state of your well-being." He looked Beth over as he approached. "You look fit, I'm happy to see. Are you?"

"Tell me something, Temple" Beth responded. "How can a man talk so foggily erudite, and write a newspaper with total clarity?" She looked at him with affection. "Yes, I'm fine. Thanks for asking."

Swift tugged an ear lobe. "I can see you're fine. And I'll be giving the Lord a thank you for that. As for my speech versus my writing. You will understand that since the mouth is closer to the brain than are the fingers, it has not the time that my fingers enjoy to distill my thoughts." He grinned. "Now, for publication, give me all the gory details. This tale of yours will spice up this week's edition." He opened his pad and fumbled in his shirt pocket. "Have you a pencil I can borrow?"

Details in hand, Temple concluded, "I was taught a lesson this morning by your lovely Annie in what she called fun stuff. She has evidenced a willingness to continue the lessons. I think I'm going to enjoy the course."

Swift was scarcely out the door when a breathless Shelly Burg raced in. "I just heard. Are you okay?"

"That Dumpster sure gets around, doesn't he?" Beth returned Shelly's reassuring hug.

At Shelly's insistence, Beth retold her morning's adventure. Then, "Don't you have a restaurant to run, Shelly? Who's flipping the pancakes?"

"Don't worry. It's covered. But, I'd better get back. See you."

Beth nodded. "See you."

A parade of villagers came to the drugstore through the day, all curious, all concerned. Beth felt the warmth of it. But the Ed memories, once started, continued to press in on her.

CHAPTER TEN

Grace Jensen's knock on the front door of the tidy, one-story bungalow was answered immediately. The warm smile and eager eyes of the Rev. Oscar Petersen greeted her.

"Come in, Grace. Come in," he said, standing back and gesturing her inside.

Grace took in Oscar's tall frame, stooped now under the gravity of eighty-eight years, and gave him a hug. "You look well, Pastor," she said, and wondered again why she had never felt free enough to address him by his first name. She could hug him, but couldn't bring herself to say Oscar. Strange, she thought as she often did, how in that one way the relationship she had with him as her seminary professor remained deeply rooted.

Oscar had retired in Plum just before Grace received the call to Gethsemane Lutheran Church Uptop. She remembered how his presence in Plum was a consideration before accepting the call. Local church histories are replete with stories of pastors who retired in or near their former parishes, and who became second-guessing thorns in the sides of new pastors. Grace now thought of that concern in the light of her many years at Gethsemane. Never once had Oscar interfered. Consistently and gracefully he had always declined pastoral involvement unless it was to stand in when she vacationed.

Oscar's wife, Ingrid, joined them and set a thermal pitcher and a tray of cookies on a carved coffee table. She patted Grace's shoulder with a "Welcome, Grace," served the coffee and cookies, and settled quietly into a cushioned chair.

"Yes, so how was the meeting, Grace?" Oscar asked. It was his weekly opener after they ascertained each was in good health, that the nation was strong, Plum was healthy, and the weather unseasonable or not. Oscar had once been a regular member of the group, but no longer attended. Grace was his conduit.

"We have a new member," she replied. "His name is Fred Sweeney, a Roman Catholic archbishop no less. But you would never guess it by the sight of him. He wears jeans and a sport shirt. He is afflicted by Lou Gehrig's disease and lives his days in a scooter-type wheelchair."

"Do you like him?"

Grace knew the underlying question asked if Fred was a man of God. "I do," she replied. "Perhaps I should say I have a favorable initial impression. He was a listener at the meeting and made only a few comments, but they revealed an ability to look critically at his own church."

Oscar raised his eyebrows. "Yes. So, can you look critically at your church, Grace?"

"If I didn't before, I will be called to do so shortly. The meeting turned to a challenge prompted by the sad death of John Plum Chase and articulated by Shelly Burg. She wanted to know why there are *three* churches Uptop, all Christian. And did those separations possibly contribute to John's taking his own life. It got all of us thinking. Does our mutual exclusion leave spaces open for people to drop through? Can we find ways to come closer? Can we ensure that all our neighbors are attended, members or not? And, how close can we get?

"Did you decide?"

"Not yet. We put it on our next agenda."

"Yes, But you've been thinking about it?"

"Since the question was raised I've scarcely thought about anything else."

Oscar picked up a pipe, looked at Grace for a nod of permission, lit it and took several puffs. "Ingrid has me down to three pipes a day," he said a bit apologetically. "But it has always helped me think, or so I tell myself. So, what are you thinking, Grace?"

"I'm glad to have you to talk to about this, Pastor. You are my pipe. You help me think better. I am concerned that I act within the scope of our Lutheran theology. Also, I voiced my concern that our three churches don't end up united, but then be just another breakaway church joining the many thousands of breakaways in Christian history."

"Yes. So, good, you've set some parameters. Are you open to changing them?"

"Not yet, I think."

"What else?"

"I ask myself, should we even get into this at a local level? Is it so bad to be different?"

"Yes. So how do you answer that?"

"In my heart I know that our long separation and all of the historical animosities are disgraceful. Christians should be one. Not to be united speaks a contradiction to our fundamental moral beliefs. So I can't argue for the status quo."

"Ah, but those animosities are real, Grace. I would bet you that every single member of our church has stories to tell, many from personal experience, others learned from family and friends. Think of all the stories you have heard about marriage between Lutherans and Catholics, the Catholic demand that all children be raised Catholic, refusals to permit ministers to concelebrate, venal demands for money to fix things. You know the list as well as I do. When I was young even children were brought into the fray. I recall walking to our public school on one side of the street while Catholic children walked to their school on the other side. We hurled taunts at one another. 'Cat-licker, cat-licker,' we'd yell. 'Pup-licker, pup-licker,' they'd answer. "Childish, but we were children."

"I know."

"And you also know, Grace, that these same animosities exist now between our own Lutheran brothers and sisters. Even though you and I are ordained ministers of the Evangelical Lutheran Church in America, we are not acceptable to other Lutheran synods."

"Yes. It all starts with acceptance, doesn't it? Acceptance and forgiveness, what you used to teach us in the seminary as the core religious reality for Christians. We are accepted, we must accept. We are forgiven, we must forgive. I feel a need to prepare our people for greater and greater reconciliation. I'll preach on it this Sunday."

Oscar puffed on his pipe. "So, it seems, Grace, you are left with the one question. What can you do at the local level, if anything?"

"As a start I will recommend to the other pastors that we get our parishioners working together on one or more of the ministries we have in common."

Oscar puffed thoughtfully. "I like that," he said at last. "If any one of your parishioners suddenly stops participating, it will pinpoint her or him as having problems, and a need for you to counsel. Our people are good, Grace, as you know. Sure they get their hackles twitching now and then like everybody else. But down under, they're good. I think you will be supported. You might start by running your ideas past Robyn. As president of the congregation, her support will be invaluable."

***

Grace felt a chill from the stethoscope as Robyn checked her heart and lungs. When the physical exam was over, she sat on a chair next to Robyn's examining-room desk.

"Overall, you look good, Grace," Robyn began, checking some papers in her hand. "Your blood tests are all in normal ranges for sugar, cholesterol, and lipids. Your heart and lungs are good. No sign now of that bronchitis. Your blood pressure is a little elevated, higher than I want to see it. And that's not you. Usually you're on the low side. Are you experiencing any new stress at this time?"

"I don't think it's stress, Robyn. I'll admit I've been preoccupied. At our pastors' meeting last week many of the townspeople came up to us and expressed guilt over John Plum Chase's death. They thought we all failed him somehow. They more or less appointed us to get on top of this so it doesn't happen again. Then Shelly Burg suggested that our divisions, I mean the three churches Uptop, may have contributed to it because of our separateness. Put together, those events got our attention. We decided to look at our differences to see how important they are. I'm not obsessing about it, but I admit it occupies my mind much of the time."

"Shelly told Beth and me about it yesterday at lunch. Are you concerned what our congregation's reaction might be?"

"Well, I do want your opinion. Oscar even suggested I talk to you."

"I'm with Shelly on this, Grace. When people walk into this office I don't check their religious affiliation. I treat them all, and I try to treat each one the best I can. How many times have you preached that God's attitude toward us is exactly that? And I try to make it my attitude. Any other way of acting would be like acne on Plum's face."

"So, you'll support me if I try to bring our congregations closer?"

"Grace, your congregation loves you. We trust you. You lead. We'll be there with you."

"Thank you, Robyn, that helps."

"Good. Now you just sit here for a few minutes, breathe deeply and think pleasant thoughts. I'll be back. We'll take that blood pressure one more time."

***

Grace stepped up into the ambo and looked out at her congregation. Feeling slightly nervous she launched into her sermon.

"Grace to you and peace from God our Father and our Lord and Saviour, Jesus Christ.

"Let us pray. Dear God, you loved us so much that you sent your Son who gave up his glory to become one of us, to teach and heal and die for us. Help us to understand your will for us. Let your Word go to our mind and heart and then our hands. In Jesus' name, Amen.

"Many of you have come to me and expressed guilt and concern over the death of John Plum Chase. All of us wonder if we could have prevented it. My response this morning begins with a story about a Southern Baptist woman from Virginia. Her name was Beatrice. I knew her at the University in Stockford. She would spend summers there with her son, a fellow professor of my husband, Dick. She was in her nineties when I knew her. I came to respect the deep faith she had and we would often talk about our faith. One day she shared this metaphor:

"At the beginning of time three angels held globes, one globe of truth, one of love, and one of unity. The angel carrying the globe of truth dropped it, and it shattered. Pieces of glass lay all about. People ran to pick them up, thinking that they would then have truth. But they didn't have truth. They only had pieces of it.'

"My dear friends. We share this hill top with United Church of Christ and Roman Catholic congregations. Those people are our neighbors. They have their pieces of truth. Pastors Paul Staunton, Jack Tyrrell and I have talked about drawing closer to one another. We feel we all have a part to play, pieces of truth to bring, in putting the globe of truth together again.

"How will we do this? Slowly! In small steps! We must first get to know each other. Mother Teresa said, 'Most of us cannot do great things. We can only do little things with great love.' Most likely the coming week will present us no more than the chance to write a note, visit a nursing home or a jail, give blood, teach a Sunday School class, give food to the food pantry, tell a child a story or collect money for some worthy cause.

"I will suggest to Pastors Staunton and Tyrrell, as our beginning part in putting the globe of truth back together, that we begin doing some of these small things together. Just because we must work on the globe of truth does not mean that we can act as if the globe of love is broken, or the globe of unity that love brings. I would appreciate your prayerful thought on this.

"May God, who knows our hearts, help us to be faithful in our time."

CHAPTER ELEVEN

Beth opened her store with a faint sense of apprehension. She thought of locking the door while she swept the floor and straightened shelves, but decided against it. She would not bow to that one exception in Plum's tranquility. Her broom dislodged a lone vitamin bottle from under a counter. She tossed it into the wastebasket, its plasic shell cracked and bent by the weight of her pursuer. Worth the price, she mused.

She had thought it was Ed. Thoughts of her first marriage started to seep into her memory. She knew that to shun those images only gave them more power and made them more insistent, so she looked at them squarely once again, the few good memories and then the bad.

The good memories were short. They covered their courtship and first few weeks of marriage.

The rest of the memories came back as moments of uncovered deception. Her self-deception was the hardest now to reconcile. She had been taken in by the smooth surface qualities of the man. Then there was his parents' deception. "We thought you had changed him," they told her. "That's why we didn't tell you." What they had failed to reveal was their son's uncontrollable and conscienceless early behavior.

Almost from the beginning the marriage had been regularly punctuated by deceit on Ed's part, and by his increasing attempts to dominate and control her. The event that finally made her see him as a sociopath returned with all its force.

***

Ed was fired by his employer, a brokerage firm. He was accused of theft, of converting client funds to his own account. The theft was transparent. Ed had made no attempt to conceal it. After reviewing the evidence, the district attorney had no choice but to prosecute. Ed was arrested. Beth learned of it two days later from his parents. They had provided immediate bail, and an attorney for Ed.

"Why didn't you tell me?" she asked at breakfast, after a sleepless night. "I'm your wife."

"I didn't want to worry you," Ed responded, sounding considerate. "This is nothing. It's all a mistake."

Beth stared at him. Did he really believe that it was nothing? "I'll get a job to help us get through, Ed. Even if it's nothing, it'll take time to clear it up. There are plenty of jobs out there for pharmacists."

"Never!" Ed's tone changed. "By god, we'll starve first."

"But Ed, you'll need all your time for the court case. We need to live. It's doubtful at best that you will have any chance of employment as long as the charges are unsettled."

"Never!" he shouted.

"How will we live?"

"My folks have money."

"They've already done so much for us."

"Let me spell it out! You're not listening. N.E.V.E.R. spells never. Do you get it?" His voice was low and menacing.

Beth suppressed her growing anxiety. "I'm going to get a job, Ed," she said softly. "I'm going to get a job today."

Ed stood, reached across the table and struck her with a closed fist. "You're not leaving this house, period!"

Shocked, Beth stood up, her palm covering her cheek.

Ed came around the table, grabbed her by the wrist and pulled her to the basement door. He flipped on the basement lights and dragged her down the steps. "You'll stay here, by god, until you get it. Got it? You're not leaving this house!" He turned, walked up the stairs and slammed the door.

Beth heard scraping sounds at the door. She went to try it. It wouldn't yield. He had wedged something against it. She turned back down and tried to clear her mind. The lights went out. The darkness was total in the windowless space. She gently touched her bruised cheek, then sat on the bottom step as tears began to flood her face. It was some time before she became conscious of the cold. She hugged herself for warmth, but it was not enough to stop the shivering. She lost all sense of time. Darkness must do that to time, she thought. The cold and the darkness helped her think, gave her thoughts clarity. She tried the door again, same result. From time to time she could hear Ed moving about above her.

At one point her need to urinate became insistent. She knocked on the door. "Ed, I need to pee! Ed?" There was no response. She remembered a stack of flower pots and rummaged blindly to find them. She took one and relieved herself.

Her imagination colored and vitalized long forgotten memories. She saw herself at age eleven on the school playground, skinny, the peewee of her fifth grade class. The playground rang with kids' clamor. Mae and Alice had the jump rope swinging as Beth timed her entry. Suddenly a push from behind sent her into the rope and onto the pavement. Rotten Ronald sneered, "You were in my way, runt." Beth looked at her bleeding knees, then up at Ronald's fleshy hulk. She was suddenly a fury hurtling herself into his soft belly, her right fist flying upward. The fist caught Rotten Ronald on the bottom of his nose. He plopped down of his own accord, his two hands covering his nose, blood oozing out between his fat fingers, his eyes cowed and anxious.

Beth moved up, bent and wiped snot from her fist onto Rotten Ronald's shirt, then turned and walked away.

Standing before the school principal she was defiant. "He's a bully, and I ain't gonna be bullied never."

"I'm not going to be bullied ever, Beth," the principal corrected. It became a grammar lesson. The principal turned discipline over to her parents.

"We'll see what dad has to say," her mother said.

Her dad sat in his easy chair that evening as Beth stood before him and related her tangle with Rotten Ronald.

"Beth, I'm proud of you. You did the right thing." He stood up and punished her with a hug.

When the basement lights went on she squinted to adjust her eyes, then looked at her watch. She had been there for eight hours.

The door swung open and Ed stood at the top of the stairs. "You can come up now, Beth," he said coldly.

Beth climbed the stairs warily, her eyes on Ed.

Ed stepped back as she entered the room. "I'm guessing you learned a lesson," he said.

Beth sidled away from him. "Yes, Ed, I've learned a lot." She looked at the kitchen clock to avoid his eyes. "I'd better get dinner. I picked up a nice beef tenderloin yesterday. You go relax and watch TV while I get it all together." She watched him nod agreement and leave the kitchen, then heard the voice of a TV market analyst.

She made the dishes clatter as she set the table. Then she made a salad and put it in the refrigerator, scrubbed two baking potatoes and set them next to the stove. She trimmed the silverskin from the tenderloin, put it in a baking pan, and back into the fridge. Turning the oven on, she placed the potatoes onto the center rack. At the cupboard she pulled out an old brown ceramic cup and emptied it into her hand. She counted the bills, nineteen dollars plus change.

Beth walked into the living room. "Dinner's in the oven, Ed, except for the tenderloin. I've got time to run down to the corner for a bottle of merlot. Is that okay with you?"

Ed responded with a casual wave of his hand.

Beth put on her coat, a stocking cap and boots. She wrapped a scarf around her neck, walked past Ed and out the front door. She left her car in the garage for fear the sound of the engine would alarm Ed. Out of vision from the house she started to run. Ten minutes later, exhausted from alternately walking and running through the residential area, she got lucky. A passing cab had dropped its passenger farther up the street and stopped at her frantic waving. Twelve dollars poorer she rang the bell at Robyn's apartment door. Be home, she prayed, please be home. She rang again. When there was no answer, she sank to the floor, her back against the door. Tears came in streams. She felt the collapse of her world, and imagined a barren and cold future. She pulled the collar of her coat tighter, chilled even in the warm corridor.

Robyn arrived twenty minutes later, pulling her winter jacket from her white uniform. She helped Beth to her feet and hugged her.

Inside the apartment, seated on the floor before a fire, Beth told the entire story. She'd been there about an hour when the phone rang. She listened as Robyn answered.

"No, Ed, Beth's not here....No, I haven't seen her....No, she hasn't called. Why?" Robyn turned to Beth. "He hung up."

"I'm afraid of him, Robyn. How could he hit me?"

"You're safe here, Beth," Robyn assured. "As to how a man can act like that, well, I don't mean this to sound like an I-told-you-so, but in a way it's just that. I'm not a psychiatrist, but in Med School we all did our psych rotations. I met other Eds there. They're people who have little or no capacity for emotions. Guilt is limited or not there at all. They can be real sweet, or real mean, and not feel really good about the one or guilty about the other. And they don't seem to have developed a conscience. They can steal and not feel guilty, and even be surprised that others are upset about it. They can fake it, but they don't feel any real sympathy for anyone. We used to call them psychopaths. I'm betting, on what you've told me, that that's Ed. And Beth, they can't be cured. So don't even think about giving it another try. Get out, and get out now."

"You said you told me so?"

"I tried to point things out after the double dates we had, things like his lack of the usual courtesies for you and his obvious sense of being superior. I never believed for once any of those bragging stories he brought back from his vacations. But, I wasn't sure about him either. And you, well, Jesus Christ couldn't have convinced you there might be a flaw in the guy. Am I right?"

Beth nodded.

***

Beth stayed at Robyn's apartment for two weeks. Her decision to file for divorce was firm. She located and was hired for a pharmacist position after her first interview. Just as quickly she found and moved into an apartment in the northern suburb of Glenview, close to her work and a healthy distance from the home she had shared with Ed. She obtained an unlisted telephone number.

Robyn had several encounters with Ed. "He was waiting outside my apartment. He's obsessed, Beth. It's a cold hate, but it oozes out. He's determined to find you."

"What did you tell him?"

"To get lost."

At his latest encounter with her, Robyn reported to Beth, "He says he only wants to reach you so he can deliver your car."

"Tell him to sell it. He can bring the title to you for my signature."

"He won't do that. He sees this car as a sure link to you."

"Then tough. I don't want the car. His parents gave it to me, so I don't feel any claim on it. By the way, I've notified all those official places, the state motor vehicle department, the IRS, you name it, that I changed my address. I used yours. I hope that's okay."

"No problem. But, Beth, I'm sure he's working full time to find you."

"I know. He's been seen driving around my home town in Wisconsin. He's called my parents several times."

"Beth, watch your back."

"I will. My attorney will file divorce papers early next week. I suppose that will lead to at least one meeting with Ed, but I'll be protected there."

Two days later, Beth looked up from filling a prescription to see Ed at the counter looking at her, a triumphant gleam in his eyes.

"Hi, there," he said, sounding jovial.

Beth stared at him. A lump filled her throat, her heart pounded. She said nothing.

"You can come home now," he said, reassuringly.

"No, Ed. It's your home now. Not mine." She spoke quietly, deliberately.

"We can work this out, Beth."

"No, Ed. We can't work this out. I'm filing for divorce in a few days."

Ed's tone lost its hint of supplication. "You file for divorce, by god, and I'll show you what a fist can really do."

"I have to get back to work, Ed. We'll talk at the hearing."

"I'm a customer, goddam it, we'll talk now."

A stocky middle-aged man walked out of a back room and stood at the counter. "I'm the store owner, sir. Names's Reggie Bagley. Is there a problem?"

Ed seemed to take the measure of Bagley, then turned toward the door with a parting shot at Beth. "Remember by god, it's me, or it's bye-bye."

Beth explained the situation to her boss. "He'll be back, I'm sure, Mr. Bagley. I can't control that. If you think it's in your best interest, I'll resign today."

"You're much too good an employee, Beth. We'll find a way to control that gentleman."

Eventually, after several violations of a court order to stay clear of the neighborhood, subsequent encounters with the police, stiff fines, and a jail threat from a judge, Ed stayed away. Only later did Beth learn that the real reason was another matter. Ed's trial for theft of client funds came up. Ed was found guillty, ordered to make restitution and sentenced to one year in prison. Except for his voluminous letters written from prison, letters that entreated one time and threatened the next, Beth was given a respite.

It surprised Beth that Ed did not contest the divorce as he had threatened. She suspected that he was too busy adjusting to prison life. She felt again the freedom of the divorce decree.

***

"Mom, Mom, look what Mr. Swift and I found in the creek," Annie shouted as the door bell jangled its warning. "It's a frog." She carried it upside down, holding it with a fist wrapped around one hind leg. "I'm gonna name him Mr. Jumper. Can I keep him? Can I?

All the dark thoughts evaporated as Beth squatted to the level of Annie's bright dark eyes. "He's a beauty, Annie. Sure you can keep him. When dad gets home I'll bet he'll build a pen for Mr. Jumper. Did Mr. Swift play with you today?"

"Yah. I teached him more fun stuff."

"What fun stuff today?"

"I teached him how to twirl around until you get dizzy."

"Did Mr. Swift get dizzy?"

"Yup. He sat right down in the creek."

"Oh my. Well, you just wait behind the counter while I close the store."

She was about to turn off the lights when Jack Tyrrell came in and expressed his concern over her recent encounter. He bought a package of band-aids.

Beth thanked him and gave him change. Looking at his Roman collar as he left the store, she thought, that's the rest of the Ed story, the church part.

CHAPTER TWELVE

Smartly dressed in a pale yellow suit, Moira Quinney entered St. Anne's Church, fluffed her light brown hair, tinted and styled attractively for someone younger than Moira's fifty-two years, and walked up the center aisle to attend the 11:00 a.m. Mass. She took her place in the front left pew, directly in front of the pulpit. She mechanically followed the opening prayers of the Mass, but came fully alert when *that priest* walked to the pulpit. She clutched her purse in front of her, reached in, pushed a button, and shielded the purse opening with her palm.

Jack Tyrrell, in alb and green chasuble, walked to the pulpit to read the gospel for the day.

"A reading," he began, "from the Good News according to the tradition of Luke.

"There was a man going down from Jerusalem to Jericho who fell prey to robbers. They stripped him, beat him, and then went off leaving him half-dead. A priest happened to be going down the same road; he saw him but continued on. Likewise there was a Levite who came the same way; he saw him and went on. But a Samaritan who was journeying along came on him and was moved to pity at the sight. He approached him and dressed his wounds, pouring in oil and wine. He then hoisted him on his own beast and brought him to an inn, where he cared for him.

'Which of these three, in your opinion, was neighbor to the man who fell in with robbers?'"

Jack walked to the front of the center aisle. He grinned at a child who was distressing his parents with loud questions, and gave the parents an understanding smile.

"We will never understand Jesus," he began, "until we understand Jesus, the lawbreaker.

"In the religious culture of Jesus' time, there existed a whole range of laws that covered nearly every moment of peoples' daily lives. Should someone violate one of these laws they were considered *unclean.* They required purification before they could again be considered *clean*, and allowed once again to associate with the *clean* people. A lawbreaker was sent out, ostracized, kept out of law abiding society until he or she had gone through the purification requirements.

"Jesus broke these laws with total abandon. He violated the hugely important Sabbath laws. He defended his disciples for plucking and eating grain on the Sabbath. He healed people on the Sabbath. These were grave violations of the Sabbath law, and Jesus was *unclean* because of it.

"There were laws about washing hands so many times a day, and laws about what you could or could not eat. Jesus summed up his response: 'There is nothing outside a person that by going in can defile, but the things that come out are what defile.' He didn't worry about these laws, and was *unclean* because of it.

"In that culture you were not permitted to touch or associate with anyone considered *unclean.* Jesus did. He touched and healed the outcasts: lepers, the blind, the lame, a hemorrhaging woman. He ate and drank with these outcasts, the despised tax collectors, the wounded. And He was himself *unclean* because of it.

"Jesus lived in a patriarchal society where women were practically invisible, or who left the men *unclean* by association. Jesus' association and friendship with women made it clear that women were equals to men in His kingdom. And he was *unclean* because of it.

"In the parable of the Good Samaritan which we listened to a moment ago, the priest and Levite didn't walk past the wounded man because they were mean and uncaring. They walked past him because their laws said they would be *unclean* if they touched him. And, who did Jesus point out as being a good neighbor to the wounded man? The Samaritan, a foreigner, an *unclean* person.

"I have to tell you something folks. This guy, who we revere as having it all together, was *unclean* most of the time.

"In Jesus' mind, and in the way he lived, laws and rules and customs were for people, not the other way around. He meant also that institutions, like a church, are for people, not the other way around, not for setting up laws and rules that included some and excluded others.

"This past week we buried John Plum Chase from this very church. I often visited him, and I came to know him as a very good man. We would pray together. Because I thought I knew him and his apparent want of privacy I would then leave. It seemed the *clean* thing to do. Many of you have expressed your feelings on this, so I know I am not alone in feeling that I failed him. Am I really clean? I keep thinking that if I had stayed with him for a longer time on each visit, even in silence, that eventually the very silence might have prompted him to speak of his loneliness.

"Here at St. Anne's I propose that we take a hard look at ourselves, at those things that prevent us from being a good neighbor. Whether they be personal traits, customs or church laws, if they would exclude anyone from our company they are wrong and need changing. Are we willing to be *unclean* in the way Jesus was *unclean*?"

***

When Jack left the pulpit, Moira unobtrusively reached into her purse, pushed the stop button, and pulled a handkerchief out to dab daintily about her nose.

Back in her home, Moira flitted about her kitchen. Sunday -- Saints. Picture images of her favorite saints and purfled prayer cards with calligraphic lettering hung about the walls and on cabinet doors. A few were held by magnets to the refrigerator. Moira presented a short prayer to each saint for the power of their intercession. "Please ask God, good St. Kevin, to keep me safe from poverty and hunger; help my sons prosper and be good; and grant me a noble place in heaven. Amen." The heaven drawn for Moira in her youth by tutoring nuns and priests was a place of sainted knights and ladies who alone had a status sufficiently noble to gain entry into the divine presence. They were the nobility of God's court, and Moira grew to covet similar status. How awful, she thought for *that priest*, Jack Tyrrell, to void their church of so many statues of this heavenly and royal clan. Particularly bitter to Moira had been the return of a John the Baptist statue which she had personally donated at considerable expense. It rested now, with only herself to give it proper devotion, on her back porch. Father Jack Tyrrell! The nerve!

Her rites completed, Moira had a fleeting sense of freedom, another duty completed as she put it, and turned on the stove and put water to boil. After readjusting several magnets and prayers, she took a single egg from its carton in the refrigerator. She dropped the egg into the roiling water, and put a single slice of fortified seven-grain bread into the toaster. Timing the egg, she removed it at the proper time, retrieved the toast and carried them to the windowed breakfast nook. She ate slowly, and for a brief moment looked out, without attention, at the grandeur of the river's sweep. Her attention stayed with wandering thoughts until caught by a picture on the wall in front of her. There in a gold and walnut frame stood her husband, Fintan (Fitz), and herself in the august company of His Excellency, Bishop Stanley McIntyre. Tickets had cost five hundred dollars each, donations of course, to attend the event which honored His

Excellency on the occasion of his fifth anniversary as bishop. Fitz had growled like a snarling wolf, but she had held her ground. She felt proud of that. And now, she was a regular correspondent with His Excellency.

CHAPTER THIRTEEN

There is light and shadow yet on the river's far side. Here, below the hill shade comes early. I have had a most satisfying day and I bask in the memories of it. My nose is red from sunburn, but gives me no discomfort against those memories.

Dumpster picked me up at six this morning. He exchanged his car with Felicity for our van which is equipped to take in Rover through one spacious side door. We drove to his home where I maneuvered Rover a few inches down a makeshift ramp onto the carpeted bow of his fishing boat. I sat facing the starboard, a waist high brace for a standing fisherman in front of me. Dumpster braced the scooter wheels to prevent movement, and we were off. We created the only breeze of the still morning by our movement. It was cool and pleasant.

We ran upriver for about two miles before Dumpster slowed, turned off the outboard motor, and entrusted us to the sluggish current of the river. He came forward with a rod and reel baited with a jig (I later learned) and minnow. He set the rod in my hand with its tip resting over the standing brace.

"We're gonna float," he said. "Now you just let out enough line until you feel the jig hit the bottom. Then turn the crank abour half a turn. Did you feel it when the jig hit the bottom?"

I nodded.

"Good. Just slowly raise the jig a few inches from the bottom, and then lower it back down. Keep repeating the up and down movement slowly."

He took my rod and demonstrated the movement.

"Can you work that okay?" he asked. There was a little concern in his voice.

"Yes, at least until my wrist tires," I said.

"Okay, when your wrist gets tired, use the reel. Just crank it up a turn, then release. It'll work the same. Now, let's get some fish."

I had about lost hope after Dumpster landed his third walleye pike. I was sure that I was doing something wrong. But, with that thought still in my head, a fish took my bait. I reeled as fast as I could (which was slow) against the fish's pull, and eventually brought it to the surface. Dumpster reached down and brought the fish into the boat, his thumb and forefinger holding it by a gill opening. I must say I felt triumphant. I had never caught a fish, or anything else, and now I had this in common with all the food gatherers of all time. I was a buffalo hunter, a harpooner of whales. When I looked at the fish I watched it transmute into two luscious fillets. Dumpster cleaned the fish as we caught them.

I caught three more walleyes before Dumpster called a halt. He wanted to give me a tour, he said. We zipped further upriver for five or six more miles. From time to time he would slow the boat and shout over the motor noise, "That's the Ryan place," or "Doc Robyn and her husband own that farm," and "I was raised on that one."

Back down river Dumpster pulled off into the slough opposite the village. He stopped the boat in a quiet pond.

"It's time for lunch," he said.

I watched with fascination as he set up a small two-burner stove on the middle seat, and put a skillet on each burner. He placed two huge potatoes and an onion on a kind of chopping board on his lap, peeled and sliced them, and swiped them with his palm into a buttered skillet. They were sizzling in no time. Then he reached into the cooler and displayed a handful of fillets. "How many?" he asked.

"Just one for me," I said. Three went into the other skillet.

Dumpster was quiet as he worked. My attention shifted back and forth, to Plum across the waters, to the idyllic scene about me where white egrets and great blue herons hunted along the shores, to Dumpster at work.

"Beer or coffee?" he asked.

"Beer, please."

He poured two beers into paper cups. Next he took the skillet of potatoes and divided its contents onto two paper plates and added the fillets. He put a beer onto the chopping board along with a plate and brought it to me. He set the tray on my lap and stuck a straw in the beer.

"Will that work?" he asked.

"Yes," I replied.

We ate in silence for a while and then Dumpster began to talk about the places he had pointed out upriver.

"That last place belonged to my aunt and uncle, Rachel and Hiram," he said. "They raised me there. When they died, I got the place, me and Becky..."

He told me then the story of his life with Becky. I was surprised, but pleased, at this display of trust.

"You think she'll come back someday?" he asked.

"I can't read the future, Dumpster," I said, "but I'll pray for it."

"I was hopin' you would."

When we got home I triumphantly took the remaining fillets to Felicity in the kitchen. "I caught these," I said proudly.

Felicity took the fillets and held them to her nose. "They smell fresh," she said. "I do believe they really are fresh, and since you were with Dumpster I know you didn't get them at the grocery store."

"I appreciate your confidence," I said.

She walked by me to the refrigerator. "But you don't smell fresh," she said as she passed by. Her eyes were mischievous when she returned from despositing the fillets. She faced me from in front of Rover. "You stink fish," she said. "I'll call Cory and get you a bath. Then I might boil your clothes."

I could hear her chuckling as I drove to my study. Clearly I can't pass myself off as Queequeg from the Pequod in this house.

***

I was unable to make the pastor's luncheon today. Yesterday I experienced a small respiratory problem. Both Maggie and Felicity turned it into an emergency. Maggie kept a hawk-like vigilance over me throughout the day, and, I suspect, the night. I confess that I have missed her presence when she spends such long days at the university. Even on week-ends we seldom get a chance to talk. Yesterday we talked and I showed her the small journalings I've done. She read them and we discussed them. Despite my small breathing discomfort I wouldn't trade a day like that for anything.

This morning Felicity had me at Dr. Robyn Horsager's office when it opened. Doc Robyn, as everyone seems to call her, did a brief check of my vital signs and then sent me over to the hospital at Stockford for tests. Felicity tore over the roads. When I called her a lead-foot Franciscan, she only went faster.

When the tests were completed we raced back to Robyn's office for a noon hour exam based on the tests. I have a feeling of great confidence in her medical skills. She ordered a prescription for me from the Plum Pharmacy and will see me again at my scheduled appointment next week. She also prescribed physical therapy and had the receptionist schedule an appointment with Cory.

I have been at my desk since our return. Felicity served our lunch here in my study. I eat slowly, but heartily, with a lessened ability to swallow.

"What looks like pepper on your smoked turkey is actually arsenic," she said. "A small payback for your lead foot remark."

"I thought it tasted better than usual," I responded. "Not to worry though. We habituate our bodies to arsenic in the seminary. It's a hangover from the medieval papacy when poisonings were in fashion. Did you ever cook in a seminary?"

My reading was interrupted about 2:30 this afternoon. I heard the doorbell and the murmur of feminine voices when Felicity opened the door. She appeared at my study with Grace Jensen in tow.

"Come in Grace," I said, indicating one of the leather chairs. "How nice of you to come." I turned Rover so that I faced her.

"The group sends you their prayers and good wishes, Fred. Dumpster told us that you were ailing. How are you, really?"

"I'm fine, Grace, thank you. Doc Robyn has me all patched and oiled. How did the meeting go today? I was looking forward to being there."

"The meetings are always fun. And it went well. Paul, Jack and I agree that we would begin our movement toward greater unity by having our parishioners join together in some of the ministries we have in common: visiting shut-ins, providing them transportation to doctors and hospitals, things like that. The three of us are meeting later this week to select the first services that we will do together. It's a small step perhaps, but it's a step."

"I think your small step may only look small. It might span the entire distance. I only wish I could be more active in helping the three of you, and Dumpster."

"You shouldn't underestimate the value of your support," she said.

It was kind of her to say that. If I succumb to resentment about my illness at times, it's to do with a feeling of uselessness. "Thank you," I replied. "You've buoyed my spirits. Earlier today, I was surfing the net to find out more about the Evangelical Lutheran Church in America. I was pleased to see how close we are in so many ways. An article by one of your seminary professors told of how the freedom Christ has brought us is a freedom to be for others. It ties in so well with these beginning ministries in common."

Grace told me of her children and their current occupations and locations. She is a grandmother many times over. She preached the other Sunday on the joint and joining efforts of the three parishes, and she has promised me a copy.

***

A busy day indeed. (The phrase reminds me of a pastor I knew as a young priest who felt oppressed and weary, and complained bitterly of his heavy work load, after a day's work of a half dozen phone calls.) Within an hour of Grace's departure came another doorbell and another smattering of feminine voices. This time Felicity escorted Beth Halkerston, our Plum pharmacist, to my study. Beth had in hand Robyn's prescription for me.

"I brought it over because there are a few cautions about this medication," she began. "Also, because I wanted to meet you," she said cheerfully.

I thanked her for coming in person and expressed my hope that she had not been hurt in the recent attack upon her person.

"You heard about that?" she asked.

I nodded. "Yes." Her instructions on the medication were as direct as her opening words to me. I liked her immediately. When she finished, she sparked my curiosity by getting up and closely examining a carved crucifix on the wall near her chair.

"Are you a Catholic, Beth?" I asked.

"I used to be."

"You didn't find it nourishing?"

"I was kicked out."

"Can you talk about it?"

"Sure..." She talked in a rush, the whole story of a failed marriage.

I won't repeat the private details in this account. What is public is her divorce and her subsequent appeal to the Church for an annulment. The annulment was granted her at the local diocesan level, but was appealed to the Vatican by her ex-husband (a genuine sociopath according to the psychologists that investigated the matter). The Vatican overturned the local decision, a most unusual move. Beth told me of a mocking call from her ex-husband from Rome, where he had gone to oppose the annulment. He knew the decision before her local bishop did. I suspect he charmed or paid tribute to someone in the Vatican. "Do you even want to be a Catholic after all that?" I asked.

"Yes," she said without hesitation. "I miss it, the smells, the bells, all of it."

"May I see if I can do something for you?" I asked.

"Sure. I'm not begging though. I won't give up my husband and family for it. My conscience is clear when it comes to my re-marriage. And I won't be a second class Catholic, one who has to sit in the back pews and can't take communion."

"Does Jack know about this?"

"Not that I know of."

"May I bring him into the picture? I will need his help."

"Sure."

After Beth left, my mind was caught up in this whole annulment process of the Church. It's Catholic divorce, really. And it's nonsensical. We Catholics have far to go to be as inclusive as our Protestant friends. We even exclude our own. And for what? For a human mistake! We don't exclude serial killers, or serial sex offenders. Yet, we would hold someone to a marriage bond when that marriage is obviously dead. And the underlying arrogance is the magisterial claim that "dead" is something to be determined by clerics from written statements of the parties and witnesses, and not a decision to be made within the conscience of the person in whose being lies the total experience of the marriage.

Is there a marriage? Was there ever a marriage? Only Beth should make that judgment. And even if she would err, there is no reason to exclude her. I think our church leadership has much human suffering to answer for in its reach for power and control.

I've called Jack. We'll get together on this. In retrospect, I'm surprised and pleased that Beth would open up so readily to me on this matter. Perhaps that's another reason why she brought the prescription personally.

CHAPTER FOURTEEN

Felicity set a plate of eggs, bacon and toast in front of Maggie, the same for herself, and a bowl of oatmeal for Fred. "Do you want me to puree your oatmeal?" she asked, a wicked mischievousness in her look.

"Will that make it taste better?" Fred replied innocently.

"Probably not. I hear that smart mouths aren't capable of good taste."

"That must be hard for you, then," Fred said sympathetically.

"Do you know what I think, Maggie?" Felicity didn't wait for a reply. "I think it would have helped the rest of us if his ALS had started in his mouth. Now it looks to me as if his tongue will be the last muscle to go. Woe is us."

Maggie tried to hide her enjoyment of their banter. "Will you two stop already! Eat your breakfast, both of you. If you recall, we planned this breakfast together to consider what equipment might facilitate movement and communication for Fred. If you can eat and get serious for a few minutes, we'll get at that."

"I looked at all those brochures you gave me," Fred said. "Maybe we could start with one of those feeding tubes. That way I could bypass taste."

Felicity flung a dish towel at him. "You never had it so good."

Maggie rapped a knife handle on the table. "Could we have a little order here?"

"Hear, hear," Felicity said.

"Let's flip a coin. Order or chaos," Fred said.

Maggie ignored them and spent a few minutes eating and going over the brochures she had given each of them. "Since we're on the topic of food, we'll start there. Fred, the decisions are yours. Did you see anything that might be helpful?"

"I can still swallow okay, Maggie. But, as you've both witnessed, I've been dropping a fork or spoon once in a while. Maybe one of those gloves that hold the utensil?"

"I'll order that today," Maggie said. "What about equipment for your rooms?"

"That overhead book holder for reading when I'm in bed looks good. I don't sleep as well as I used to. The book holder comes with an automatic page flipper. That looks good too. Raising my arms is getting to be a problem."

"That goes on the list then."

"Do you think it's time to get yourself a voice-operated word processing program?" Felicity asked. "You spend so much time on the computer."

"Not yet, I think," Fred replied. "I can still tap out the letters with my two-fingered method. And with a rolling dolly under each wrist I can still get to all the keys readily. It might be a good idea to get a tutorial on it though. Also I think we might get literature and a tutorial on that system that lets a person operate the computer with eye movement. That way I can be ready for both programs when I need them."

"Done," Maggie said. "Can you think of anything else?"

"We talked about a remote control for the environmental systems. I think that could save both of you a lot of steps and the trouble of responding to my needs of that kind."

"We're ahead of you there, Fred," Maggie said. She looked at Felicity who nodded. "We were going to surprise you. The system is on its way. Next week, I hope. You will be able to control all switches - lights, T.V., computer, heating, cooling, you name it, with a remote. One on Rover and one for your wrist at night. Each remote will have a button for each function that you can operate by either a push or by voice."

"I'll be living in the lap of luxury," Fred said, taking a final bite of toast. "Thank you both. Now I'm off to my day at the office." He backed Rover from the table and drove from the dining room.

Maggie looked at Felicity. Both women's eyes filled.

"Do you think I'm too rough on him?" Felicity asked.

"No, Felicity. We can't tiptoe around Fred in any way. He loves jousting with you. The more pointed the lance, the better. He needs, and we need to support, his independence as much as we can."

***

Rover and I took a slow tour of main street this afternoon. I had banking to do. Maggie and Felicity have delegated me the responsibility for our common account. I had been to the Plum bank before, but today a gentleman I had not met saw me at the counter and stepped out from his office.

"My name is Marvin Principle, Sir," he said. "You're the new reverend here in town, I'm told. Well, we will take good care of your money, rest assured of that, Sir. And we're mighty pleased to have your business."

"I'm Fred, Marvin," I responded. "I'm pleased to meet you and I'm confident our funds are secure with you." Marvin invited me into his sparsely, but expensively appointed, office. His picture, above his bronze embossed name and designation as *President and Principal* was prominently placed just outside the door. A replica hung behind his desk. On the other three walls were portraits of J.D. Rockefeller, J.P. Morgan and Henry Ford.

I had little need of speech. For half an hour, Marvin held forth on his own humble beginnings and his rise in the world thanks to "strict moral values."

He used the kind of cliches that blend together like a collage of family pictures. "I say it like it is," and not the less assured "I say it like I see it. I can look a man in the eye and tell you if he's made of good moral stuff. Saved me some bad loans, I can tell you."

I wondered what my eye revealed.

"I'm not a very tolerant man. Too much tolerance going around. Too much goody, goody jibberish if you ask me. When you're asked to tolerate sexual deviates, sinners of any kind, you've gone too far, I say. Don't get me wrong. I believe in helping my neighbor, but I don't see throwing money down a rat hole."

Listening to Marvin I found myself thanking God for our diversity, and for loving us regardless of our eccentricities. I like Marvin. He's a good enough person, a man who holds himself and his world together with the glue of judging himself and his neighbor by standards of a world according to Marvin. As long as he controls that world, and as long as the world acts in tune with his vision, he'll do just fine.

***

In Danni's bedroom Mary watched as Danni tried on several new tops. "I really like that khaki shirt, Danni," she said. "I like them all."

"That's the end of them," Danni said. "We should go over to Stockford one of these days and do some shopping."

"That'd be fun," Mary said as she stripped and pulled her nightie over her head.

Danni watched Mary and then did the same.

"Danni, do you remember when you told me about going all the way with a boy last year? You said it didn't do anything for you."

"I remember. And it sure didn't. Why?"

"Well, like I told you, I've never been much attracted to guys. And I've wondered if something was wrong with me. You know. So last week, after the dance, I did it too."

"You did? With who?"

"Joe Bono."

"That's the same guy I did it with."

"You never told me that. I wonder if he has a trophy room somewhere?"

"Yah, right."

"So, how'd you feel about it, Mar?" Danni asked.

"Same as you said. I didn't feel anything. It wasn't warm, you know, it wasn't exciting. I sort of felt like a mattress."

"Yah, I know the feeling."

Mary was thoughtful for a while. "Did you ever talk to anybody else about it Danni? You know, about not being attracted to boys?"

"I needed to talk to somebody about it," Danni said. "So I talked to Hannah Stuart."

"How'd she react?"

"She was wonderful. She told me to give it time, but not to fret either way. Sexual orientation, she called it, doesn't have a thing to do with being bad or good. She said everybody's a good person regardless of their orientation. We should just accept ourselves. I came away feeling so good."

"I'd be afraid to talk about it. I mean, with anyone but you, Danni. You should have heard my Dad when Pastor Staunton talked about accepting gays and lesbians."

"Your dad's a wonderful guy, Mar. He loves you like crazy. Maybe you're not giving him enough credit."

"Did you ever talk about how you feel with your mom, about being attracted to girls, not guys?"

"Yah, Hannah said I should. She told me I had a great mom, that she'd understand."

"Did you?"

"Yah. And she was with me all the way."

Mary stood by the bed, unsure about her feelings, unsure about a direction to take.

"You can talk to me anytime, Mar." Danni moved close and kissed Mary lightly on her lips.

Mary felt the warmth spread into her cheeks and neck -- and reached for more.

***

Moira Quinney marched up the center aisle for Sunday Mass and stopped short at a "Reserved" sign hung on the left-side front pew, her pew. Feeling put upon by this unexpected assault on her assumed prerogative, she backed down the aisle until the fifth pew offered her asylum. She knelt but her silent prayers were muddled by imaginings of possible cause for this affront. The imaginings turned to serious questions when Beth Halkerston led her husband and three children to the reserved pew. My Lord, thought Moira, Beth Halkerston, a divorcee, in the front pew? What will that Tyrrell do next? Unable to concentrate, Moira went on automatic pilot. Kneel. Stand. Sit. She did remember to record the sermon.

When Jack was finished preaching Beth led her three children and husband into the sanctuary where Jack waited by the baptismal font. Moira began making mental notes. From the second pew, Beth's family was followed by Shelly Burg and Dumpster Heap, who stood behind Beth's two boys, and Temple Swift, who stood behind Annie. Moira's eyes widened. Dumpster Heap? A godparent? Why! Why! He's not even Catholic. Well! What else can we expect from *that priest*? Later she watched Beth and her entire family take communion. Well! What next?

At home after her breakfast, Moira picked up her empty plate and utensils and put them into the dishwasher, and refreshed her coffee. She left the kitchen and returned to its nook with a box of stationery. She began a letter to her eldest son, John. John was sixteen when they had lost Fitz to a heart attack eight years before. Fitz had been the local doctor, a mover and shaker in the county, and much respected. She still lived, wealthy and respected, under the umbrella of his memory.

> *Dear Johnny, since your father died, as you know, I have been completely disconsolate.*

Her last years with Fitz had not been comfortable. He drank to excess and communication between them gradually dwindled. He had left her in every way but public. At home he had grown callous in his desertion. The few words he uttered to her were usually mean and degrading. Moira's public tears at his wake and funeral had been tears of relief.

> *You and your brother, Jeremiah, and the Church, of course, are my only consolations. I thank God every day that you are enjoying your graduate years at the University of San Francisco.*

When John was in his senior year at High School, he and a male companion had been found in an unmistakably sexual encounter. Upon graduation, John had escaped the narrow confines of Plum and the pained remnants of his mother's bewilderment. He fled to San Francisco. There, much to Moira's relief, he had enrolled in this Jesuit University.

> *I am enclosing a check for you to have some special pleasure. It is so comforting for me to obtain my own meager pleasures vicariously through you and Jeremiah. And I am so pleased to have released you into the loving and competent hands of God and the Jesuits. I remember you daily in my prayers and sufferings. With Love,*
>
> *Mother*

A stark, forbidding sketch of the prophet, Jeremiah, and one of a crazed and wild John the Baptist elicited prayers for the well-being of her sons.

> *Dear Jeremiah, Are you too busy to come visit your poor, aging Mother?*

Jeremiah had received his bachelor's degree a year ago from Loyola University in Chicago, and had then taken a teaching position in Appalachia. Moira received a dutiful letter from him each month. She regularly sent money and complaining notes. He never answered the question about being busy, and never came. Still Moira posted him among the living saints for his unflagging devotion to the poor.

I'm a servant too, Jeremiah, as you know. Like you. Like Jesus. I give my all to my sons and to the Church. What is it in me that makes me so giving?

The thought gave her a kind of chill. She enclosed a check and sealed the letter, then took the letters and walked into her living room. She patted a wrinkle down on a lace doily and recalled its purchase in Chantilly in better days with Fitz. I love this house, she thought. She and Fitz had designed it in those better days. Twin gabled and two storied, it had four tall, white columns on its colonial-style portico. Ivy had secured tendrils in the mortar of the red brick surface and now covered the entire exterior.

My Lord, she thought. I forgot. Wednesday -- water, and I forgot. She put the letters down and watered her indoor plants. It took ten minutes.

The lawn and gardens were cared for by a service. Thursday -- tulips. In late fall each year, on the Thursday closest to Halloween, Moira herself donned white gloves and a stylish white coverall, and planted a small bed of tulip bulbs.

Moira walked into the master bedroom to get a sweater. She felt a chill. The bedroom was on the first floor, as were a large living room, dining room, kitchen and Moira's study, once the family den. The house was kept immaculate by the combination of little use and the weekly visits of another service. It was richly carpeted with orientals. The furniture was dark and expensive.

Sweater on, Moira went to her desk in the study. She put stamps on the envelopes to her sons, and then picked up and reread a letter from His Excellency, Bishop McIntyre.

Dear Mrs. Quinney:

Thank you for the intelligence on St. Anne's Parish in Plum. Your keen perception in this matter is most appreciated. May I call your attention to the presence in your fair village of His Excellency, Archbishop Frederick Patrick Sweeney. The Archbishop is a classmate of mine from the seminary, and was an international figure in the Church. It is a great loss to the Church that he has been stricken with a terminal disease.

Nonetheless, I recommend him to you. Please use my name in contacting him. I am sure that he will be a comfort to you, and an ally in seeing that our Church is run according to the rules of the Holy See.

With benevolent regard, I remain,

+Stanley McIntyre

Bishop of Rockford

Moira knew, of course, that Archbishop Sweeney had taken up residence down the street, but had struggled with an appropriate method of introduction. Now, she had one. Should she call for an appointment? No, no. Better to stop by with a small welcome gift, perhaps a vintage bottle of Italian wine. He had been living in Rome, you know. Also, perhaps, a cute little note. She would have to work on that.

His Excellency might just be the help she needed to halt these iconoclastic incursions of Father Tyrrell.

That evening, Moira drove to the Turnover for dinner. Inside she presided as a solitary presence at "Fitz's table," nodding now and then to acknowledgments from passing patrons.

Shelly Burg stopped by the table and greeted her with a cheery, "Moira, you look elegant as always."

Moira smiled her appreciation. Normally the conversation wouldn't go much beyond that, but today Moira was keen to know. "Michelle, *what* was that all about at Mass this morning?"

"You mean the Halkerstons?"

"Of course I mean the Halkerstons."

"Beth and Chuck have joined the parish, and they had their kids baptized."

"And they received communion, too," Moira added. "I thought she was divorced?

"She was."

"But...but how?..."

"I guess you'd have to ask Fred or Jack."

"Fred?"

"Yes, Archbishop Sweeney. He prefers to be called Fred.

Moira forgot to ask about Dumpster. If *His Excellency* was involved, she thought it must all be according to Hoyle. Still...

At home at her desk, Moira rewound the tape in the recorder and listened for a second time to Tyrrell's last several homilies, this time to ensure his words were audibly captured above the coughs and baby cries. Satisfied, she addressed a large envelope to His Excellency, Stanley

McIntyre. She then took a sheet of her specially engraved stationery:

> *Your Excellency:*
>
> *As you requested, I am enclosing a tape. This morning's Mass contained an event that puzzles me....*

***

Emily Martin fretted among the oval garden spaces of her front lawn. Her husband dead and her children spread to the four winds, these flowers were now her wards. She fertilized, watered, and gave them a daily dose of affectionate words. And they responded with a flourish and brilliance that brought her respect and attention from Plum's residents, respect she years ago drew vicariously from her children's academic and athletic successes.

On this day, however, she had no encouraging words for her blooms. She was herself captured by thoughts and images that filled her mind, troubled thoughts, disturbing images. Her flowers lacked power today. Not even the abundant display of yellow tea roses could elicit her full attention, or give her joy.

I've got to do something, she decided. I can't just tend my flowers and let Pastor Grace walk into a trap, or worse. She's such a beautiful person, but just too trusting -- like these begonias.

Emily walked back into her home. What should I wear she wondered as she removed a denim apron. In her world, even a trip to the grocery store demanded proper dress, not fancy, but decent and proper.

***

Emily's wide eyes were apologetic when Grace greeted her at the parsonage's front door.

"I'm so very sorry to bother you, Pastor Grace," Emily said. "I know how busy you are, and to have you take your precious time to talk to me seems so unfair."

"Emily, Emily," Grace said kindly. "I am delighted to see you anytime. Come in, please." Grace led the diminutive and elderly Emily to a chair in her office, and sat opposite. "Why, you're trembling, Emily. Are you troubled?"

Emily took a deep breath. She leaned forward, her voice unsure and whispery. "I don't like to tell tales out of school, Pastor, but after your sermon about getting closer to those other churches, I just had to come and warn you. I...I know some very bad things about Catholics. And it's from my own experience so I know it's true."

Grace's caring look went straight to Emily's eyes. Running through her mind was the sure knowledge of Emily's giving heart. She was the perpetual and faithful volunteer, generous and self-effacing to a fault. And despite her self-effacing manner, she was a leader among the women of the congregation. She could pull a female force together for any task. To divulge whatever was forthcoming was a stressful weight on the frail woman. "It's all right to share those bad things with me, Emily. I won't repeat them."

"I know you wouldn't, Pastor Grace. But you can if you want to...if it helps."

"What sort of bad things, Emily?"

"Years ago my Aunt Pamela, who was a Lutheran, went to marry George Watkins, who was a Catholic. She had agreed with George to be married in the Catholic church. When they went to see the priest, he told her that she would have to sign a paper promising to raise any children as Catholics. Well now, neither Aunt Pamela nor George wanted that. They intended for their children to make that decision themselves, when they got old enough. In the meantime, though, they were going to give those kids exposure to both churches. Well! The priest refused to perform the wedding ceremony. Even so, Aunt Pamela didn't bend an inch. She and George were on their way out of there when the priest allowed as how he might bend the rules for a hundred dollars. Can you imagine that? Well! I can tell you that got George's dander up something terrible. He stomped out of there in disgust and promptly joined the Lutheran Church. And they were good Lutherans all their life. But! Can you imagine that priest?"

"Yes, I can imagine him, Emily," Grace responded calmly. "Do you think all priests are like that?"

"I guess...well, I don't know."

"Neither of us would ever accept the treatment that one priest gave your Aunt Pamela. Even if there was one such priest, or a hundred, does that make them all bad? I know some wonderful priests. Father Jack Tyrrell is one of them. And did you know that our Church and the Catholic Church have removed all condemnations of each other. Some of those were awful and very bitter, and they lasted for hundreds of years. And we've come to agree on some very important theological matters."

"I...I don't know. I do find it hard to trust them."

"Emily, some of our own Lutheran synods won't let us take communion in their churches. Shouldn't we try to turn things around?"

"Well, I...I just wanted you to know."

"And I'm glad you did. We'll both keep our eyes open as we go along. You be sure and let me know if anything troubles you. Will you do that?"

"You know I will, Pastor Grace."

"And, Emily, let's be sure to keep our hearts open as well."

CHAPTER FIFTEEN

JOURNAL - July 19

My days in Plum are falling into a routine. Mostly I muse. I live in my head. I suspect that many of us are pushed by our aging toward a deeper search for meaning. In my own case, I'm confident my ALS intensifies the search.

I begin my day with prayer. Not a litany of recitations and requests, but a conversation. I present my insights and my questions, and challenge God to come out from hiding, enlighten and support my probing.

After prayer I read, the choices determined by the hunt of the moment. There is much wisdom available, not the least of which I find in novels. Perhaps that is why Jesus wrapped his message in stories. My meditation flows from my reading. Sometimes I nod off and wake with new insight.

If there is time left in the morning I make my notes in this journal. More often that not I get so absorbed in a book that noon arrives with no journal entries. Sometimes, though, I will take up the task in the late afternoon.

Except for the pastors' luncheon on Mondays, my noon meal during the week involves a pleasant verbal sparring with Felicity. Maggie is with us for the evenings and on the weekends. At dinner our verbal sparring is raised a notch or two by her presence. In so many ways I am a student at their feet.

In the afternoons, weather permitting, I roam about the village on Rover. I meet many people and consciously force myself to rise above my habitual social anxiety and talk to them. My tongue is often hesitant in casual conversation, but I persist and am getting better at it. I have yet to encounter meanness in anyone.

After dinner, Felicity has reserved herself an hour for private prayer. Maggie, whose prayers consume her time on the commuter, spends that hour with me. I share my thoughts of the day and she rebuts, massages or concurs with them. That hour with her is the jewel of the day's twenty-four.

My musings for this morning: It is curious to me that our religion has philosophical rather than psychological underpinnings. The message of Jesus is all about relationships. "By this will all men know you are my disciples, that you love one another." (John 13:35) How did it ever happen that religious practice wound its history ever toward belief and beliefs? How did intellectual assent to creeds come to take precedence over love of neighbor as the mark of spirituality? Why Aristotle's "Metaphysics" and its abstractions instead of his "Nicomachean Ethics" where love is to be for others for their own sake? Why defense of dogmatic lists and the theologies surrounding them instead of a search for the psychological impediments to caring, and ways to overcome them?

The answers to the 'why' of it are lost in the mists of history, and answers can only be speculative. But I would wager that we were led in that direction by generation after generation of church leaders. It was in their self-interest. As I reflect on it, I was one of them. Was it some unconscious defense mechanism in me that kept me unaware? It was so much easier to teach this or that dogma than to be unselfishly for others. After all, I counted myself a "Defender of the Faith." To be an example of a caring human being, a pedagogue of love's specifics, to get down with the disabled, the ragged and the dispossessed left sparse room for self-aggrandizement and honorific titles. It is much more comfortable preaching faith in lists than it is practicing justice.

Our Catholic history is replete with the credal 'purity' of the clerical hierarchs (how sad the term hierarchy). My own history is replete with a sometimes callous suppression of all that threatened my episcopal persona.

I don't mean to denigrate creeds. But, if creed doesn't serve love of neighbor, can it have any other value than that of transferring the primacy from love to the caretakers of creed?

***

Marvin Principle walked out of his office, a salesman's smile on his face. "Reuben Schilzgerber, come on in here," he said to a burly customer about to leave a teller's window. "I want to gab at you for a minute. You got time?"

"Sure, Marvin, I got time," the man said jovially, stuffing a small stack of bills into his denim overalls.

Once inside, Marvin closed the door and gestured toward a chair. He sat at his desk. "How are things, Reuben?" he asked.

Reuben snorted. "Hell, you know the answer to that, Marvin. Lost some of my best cows to lightning last fall. That and one more crop season like last summer's and you'll own the farm."

Even in bad times, life pulsed robustly from Reuben. "But that ain't what you want to gab about. What's up?"

Marvin hesitated. "Well, you know I got myself a little too heated at the last church cabinet meeting. I apologize for that," he said. "I've cooled down since then. But I still think Paul Staunton is leading us all down the wrong path. We can be good neighbors to people without inviting them all onto the dance floor, if you get my drift."

"I don't know, Marvin," Reuben said. "I kinda like Paul. Ain't everybody's got the guts he's got. That guy really cares about folks. We don't have to like everything he does. But, hell, his heart's in the right place. That's the way I see it."

"Well, I like Paul too." Marvin backtracked. "This isn't something personal like I've got a grudge against the man. But a change now and then is good for everybody. Paul's been with us a long time. We've pretty much heard all he's got to say. Some fresh ideas wouldn't hurt us, would they?"

"I don't know, Marvin. The devil we got could beat out the devil we might get."

"Reuben, just think about it. Okay? If you agree, well, you might get through at least one more bad year."

"I'll think about it, Marvin." Reuben's eyes grew clouded. "But, like I said, I like Paul." He stood and Marvin accompanied him to the office door.

***

The woman's voice that greeted Felicity at the door was new to me. I heard her say her name was Moira. She apologized, for some reason, for having delayed a welcome *to His Excellency.* She carried a small gift, her words, for His Excellency and a note. She hoped that someday His Excellency might favor her with an audience.

"Come in, Moira, come in," Felicity said. "Please wait just a moment and I'll check with *His Excellency.* I'm quite sure he will make time for you now."

I could picture the deviltry in Felicity's face even before she faced me at my door. "A visitor to see you, *Your Excellency*. Would you have time?"

Moments like that are hell to a man with little capacity for gesture. "Of course I have time," I replied evenly, and stuck out my tongue.

Moira Quinney is a pleasant looking woman, smartly dressed and carefully coifed. I would guess she is fiftyish. By her facial expression, I doubt that she anticipated a jeaned and T-shirted archbishop. I asked her as a favor, since I was no longer in the active ministry, to call me Fred. I told her that I felt more comfortable with that name. She seemed to understand.

I fussed over the splendid Chianti she had brought me, and read her note. "Ah, so you know Starchy? We were classmates," I said.

"Starchy? Oh! Yes. You mean Bishop McIntyre. The bishop and my departed husband and I became friends years ago. He is kind enough to correspond rather frequently."

"He's a nice man," I said, sensing that more was coming.

"Yes he is, a caring man, very much concerned about his people, about our parish too, I might add." Her tone was confessional.

"I'm sure."

"He's taken me into his confidence. He's worried about that...about Father Tyrrell."

"Really."

"You're new here, Archbishop, I mean, Fred, so you haven't seen how Father Tyrrell has systematically thrown out our Catholic traditions."

"Traditions?"

"Yes, saints. Devotion to saints. We had such wonderful statues. He got rid of them, most of them."

"Did he say why?" I sensed her rising dander.

"His reason was senseless to me. Something about needing to pay attention to what is important. Aren't saints important?"

"Of course they are," I responded. "Would you like to see my favorite saints?"

Her eyes widened. "Yes, yes I would."

I turned a portrait on my desk so she could see it. "My parents," I said. "My father was a Chicago politician, an honest-to-the-core politician. His life energies went to the well-being of the people in his district. To be such a man -- in that profession, in Chicago -- takes a saint, wouldn't you agree? I frequently ask his help. My mother also never saw a human need that she didn't try to meet. Her world was her family and her neighbors, and everyone she encountered was immediately her neighbor. I know her to be a saint, and I ask her help every day."

"Yes, of course." Consternation showed in her eyes. But, what about the great, I...I mean, famous saints?"

"For example?"

"Oh, St. John the Baptist, St. Joan of Arc, St. Therese, saints like that."

I smiled at her. "Did you know them well?"

She smiled back a hesitating smile. "Of course not."

"I like to stay with saints I've actually known. People who truly lived the gospel by loving their neighbor. Maybe it's because I've read too many of those books that sanitized the person to where I can't find a real human being. The saint that comes to mind, and I can't recall his name, was the guy who gave up his mother's milk and began fasting at the mature age of three days or so."

Moira tittered. "I've heard of that saint, but his name escapes me now also."

"Please don't misunderstand me, Moira. I think what Father Tyrrell is saying is this. We should be careful not to look upon devotion to saints as taking the place of loving our neighbor. At the same time, if that devotion nourishes us, if it helps us be better neighbors to one another, fine. Doesn't that make sense?" I could see that she was working on it.

"I...I guess I never thought of it like that."

"I think we should look upon saints as people who love us, and move away from the idea that they are 'patrons' of baking, or sore throats, or finding lost articles, or the impossible. You probably know the list better than I. Anyway, we must talk more about this another time.

"Before you go, though, we must share some of your gift. Let me get Felicity. She'll join us. You will enjoy getting to know her better. She has quite a history. University president. Head of her religious order. A list of honors that makes my head swim."

Over wine I complimented Moira on her deep interest in her faith. "I hope we can talk more in the future," I said. She seemed pleased. I like Moira. She is a prisoner of her past, like me. But she is up front about it. I'm a beginner at that.

***

Starchy McIntyre called this morning and said he'd be in the area and will stop to see me. I invited him for lunch. Shortly after the call, Jack Tyrrell rang the bell and walked in. We're saving Felicity unnecessary steps.

"McIntyre's coming to see me," Jack said, looking a bit pensive. "Says he's upset about things he's been hearing. Well, I suppose better now than later. I'm not going to hide anything."

"Starchy just called," I said. "Wants to talk to me as well." I couldn't help grinning. "You think he's got something on me too?"

Jack laughed. "I wonder who feeds his ears."

"Did he say what is your problem; I mean, his problem?"

"No."

"Well, I told him that you run with women, steal from the collections, have a violent temper, and regularly miss saying the breviary. If you're in trouble it's probably the breviary thing."

Jack howled. "You are a tonic, you old reprobate," he replied. "Can we compare notes afterwards?"

"Of course. And I know who feeds him his stuff, a good person, just misdirected. I think I might be able to redirect that person's zeal."

Jack had to leave, a meeting of the Parish Council.

"Come for dinner tonight," I said. "Felicity and Maggie would enjoy having someone intelligent to converse with for a change."

"Love to."

"Come about five. We'll talk after dinner."

Starchy arrived just before noon. Felicity did the honors and walked him to my office. After we greeted each other, did the how-long-it's-been and the weather, I asked where his driver was.

"Drive myself these days," he said. "It's the right thing to do with this priest shortage."

A small thing, I thought, but promising. There just might be some democratic parts to Starchy. "Good for you. Even as a classmate you had the common touch."

Felicity announced lunch and joined us in the dining room. Starchy spent the hour delivering appreciative phrases to Felicity for the quality of her cuisine.

Back in my office, I recited Starchy's path to glory. "Auxilliary in Chicago. Ordinary now in Stockford. Where next? An archdiocese like Milwaukee or St. Louis?"

"Not for me, Fred. If I could, I'd go back to being a parish priest. Too many problems in this job."

Score another one for the man. He looked tired. I may be guilty of misjudging him. "It's good to see you, Starchy. It's peaceful out here, restful. It might be a good place for you to get away from the stress once in a while. You're welcome any time."

"Thanks, Fred, but frankly one of my stress points is right here in Plum."

"Oh?"

"Jack Tyrrell. I lowered the boom on him this morning. One more misstep and he's in deep, doghouse doodoo."

"I'm surprised."

"He's a rule breaker. It appears he's taken it upon himself to allow a divorced and remarried woman to receive the sacraments. He said an annulment was approved by the Chicago archdiocese, but the Vatican had trouble with it. I'm going to check that out when I get back to the office.

"He took that action at my recommendation, Starchy. I know all the facts of the case. And I know you, Starchy. You'd have done the same thing." I really wasn't sure of that.

Surprise showed on Starchy's face. "Not if it breaks the rules, Fred. It sounds highly irregular."

"Yes it is, but sometimes rules don't fit the circumstances."

He stared at me. "That's another thing," he said. "Tyrrell gave a sermon that practically derided church laws. I have a tape, in fact. You know, Fred, we can't have that."

"Careful on those tapes, Starchy. It won't sit well if your priests find out they're under that kind of surveillance."

"Well," he muttered, "I've got to be vigilant."

"Look," I said, "We've been friends since our seminary days. So trust me, for a while at least. There's something going on in this small village, something good. It just might put together what Jesus was all about. I'm not going to hide anything from you, nor will Jack Tyrrell. So before you take any action, come out here from time to time, monitor what's going on here, check if rules are broken that shouldn't be. Decide then if you'd break them yourself. What harm can it do to watch and wait?"

"I'm a law and order guy, Fred."

"You're also the guy who told the seminary rector that the rule of grand silence was stupid and counterproductive."

"You remember that?" He looked pleased.

"We're getting old, my friend. We should never let ourselves be fossilized. If we would serve, we must question everything, even the rules."

"We're under a promise of obedience, Fred."

"True, but obedience can never demand that we bypass our own conscience. When we are directed to do so, it shows the inadequacy of the person demanding it."

"You'll take full responsibility?"

"Absolutely."

"Okay. I'll hold off and watch for a while. But, just so you know, I'm not comfortable."

I can picture Starchy writing a routine cover-my-butt letter to the file. As I mentally review our conversation I see clearly that laws, rules and regulations, like dogma and theologies, must be servants. They must help build up and strengthen a caring community -- or they become tools of domination.

***

I fancy at times that Rover decides the route we take on our afternoon excursions. Plum has not that many streets, and I could easily traverse every one in an hour or so. Today, though, my steed turned into a narrow lane I had not yet inspected. About halfway down the lane I came across a small cottage in the center of a lot perhaps three quarters of an acre in size. The lot is enclosed by a tall leafy hedge on all but the street side. The view of it is a breath-taking display of color. I doubt that the famed hanging gardens of Babylon could match the sight for hues. On their private lawn islands, blooms far exceeding the colors of a rainbow rose in splendor.

Completely taken by the sight I pulled to the side and stopped. Then I saw a diminutive figure stand from behind an island of tall multicolored blossoms. She was some distance away and I was about to move on from habit. Conscious now of why I avoid interaction, I stopped and spoke loudly. "You have created a treasure here," I said, "a treasury of colors."

She smiled, but it was a hesitant smile. I barely heard her faint 'thank you.'

"My name is Fred Sweeney," I continued. "I'm confined to my vehicle, or I would stand in tribute to your gardens."

Her approach was also hesitant, but she came to the roadside. "I'm Lutheran," she said. "I attend Gethsemane Evangelical Lutheran Church Uptop."

Perhaps she thought I was there to proselytize and was letting me know quietly and quickly that she would have none of it. "I've met your pastor," I replied. "She is a truly spiritual person. You are indeed fortunate."

She smiled her acknowledgment.

"May I know your name," I asked.

"Yes, my name is Emily Martin."

Emily has a decade or so on me, but is a sprightly senior. She faced me with gentle caring eyes, but wariness in their depths. She wore a wide-brimmed bonnet imprinted with a host of flowers. It was the perfect camouflage and had prevented me from spying her immediately.

"If I could walk, I'd ask you for a tour."

She thought a moment. "I'm sure the lawn will support your vehicle, Sir. And there is room for it between the islands."

"Please call me Fred, Mrs. Martin."

"I will," she said, "if you call me Emily."

Normally my memory grabs on and retains information. But Emily's instructive tour provided an overload of data. I remember words like hollyhocks, impatiens, brown-eyed susans, wild rose, etc. etc. If asked now, however, I could connect but few names with their blooms.

In the back lawn, a trellis of white roses provided shade for a table and chairs.

"Would you care for tea?" she asked.

"I would indeed, thank you."

She disappeared into the house and shortly returned bearing a tray with steaming pot, cups and saucers, and a plate of sweet biscuits. We talked. She seemed as interested in my history as I was in hers. Listening to her I wondered at the number of dedicated, caring lives lived in unheralded privacy.

When I was about to leave, Emily said she had one more garden to show me.

It lay at the back of her property shaded on the south and west by two white birch and a tall cedar-slat fence. Lilac bushes protected the north and much of the east. In area, the plot was about eight by twelve feet.

"It's my wild garden," she exclaimed. "My favorite."

I had the immediate sense that I was looking at a symbol of some inner space in Emily, an opening to adventure and to risk. Of the flowers she mentioned, many waiting for another spring to bloom, I remember May apples, trillium, and wild geranium. I remember too, and will be able to identify only jack-in-the-pulpit.

"I often come here to pray," she said.

I bowed my head with her.

***

Dumpster finished a slow patrol of the village streets and pulled onto the highway. About a third of a mile south of town he turned into the Stockford County Park, a six hundred acre mix of ponds, meadows, woods, picnic areas and sport fields. About twice a week he'd tour the park to check for vandalism on the public facilities.

He felt close to Becky here. They had come here often to hike the trails that wound through marsh, grassland and woods. He pulled to a stop in the parking lot by the river where a landing had been provided for boaters. Grabbing a clipboard from below the dash he started to pencil a letter to Becky. She had sent a letter and her address from someplace called Crete. She would be there a month. He wrote news of people she knew, but spent most of the letter describing the summer beauty of the park. "Lots of bobolinks this year."

On a far corner of the park, just away from the river, he noticed movement in the tall grass of Horseshoe Meadow. He stopped, thinking maybe a fox was out there mouse hunting. He was surprised when the flushed faces of Mary Principle and Danielle Rouan popped up into view. He got out of the patrol car. "You girls okay?"

"We're fine, Constable," Mary replied hastily. "We've been running, training for soccer. We just threw ourselves down here to catch our breath."

"Do you need a ride back into town?"

"No thanks," Danielle replied. "Our bikes are down the road a bit."

"Okay, you girls take care.

Back in his car he completed the round and drove back to Plum. Like Benjamin Franklin said, he thought, *Nor eye in a letter, nor hand in a purse, nor ear in the secret of another. It is wise not to seek a secret and honest not to reveal it.*

At the hardware store, Dumpster picked up twelve fifty-foot coils of rope and drove to the boat ramp in town. Just north of the ramp, two docks ran parallel about fifty feet out into the backwater. A boat belonging to a Turnover customer had broken loose the day before in a brisk wind. Dumpster recalled the irritated face of the customer. After rescuing the boat he had checked all the mooring lines on the docks, and found them all weather-weakened.

On the low dock, raised about two feet above the water, he took a red, swiss army knife from his pocket and cut four of the coils into sections roughly twelve-feet in length. Patiently, he wrapped tape around the ends of each piece to prevent unraveling and then tied and snugged down a line to each of the eight cleats on both sides of the dock. Moving to the high dock, raised about four feet above the water and meant for cabin cruisers, he replaced the eight fifty-foot lines with new ones. Throwing the old lines into the trunk of the patrol car he drove across the street to the Turnover's parking lot.

Inside the restaurant he took a stool at the counter as Shelly Burg put a steaming cup of black coffee at his place.

"Hi, Shelly. Got those lines changed for you. Shouldn't lose any more boats, for a while anyhow."

"Or customers, I hope," Shelly replied. "Thanks, Dumpster. That was above the call of duty."

"It was nice of you to donate the rope."

"Nice of you to change them. It's getting on toward dinner time. How about the Turnover doing your cooking this evening? Got some real nice New York Strips in today."

"I think I'll just let you do that, Shelly. Thanks. By the way, I've got some fresh walleye in the freezer. Can you and Bill use some?"

"Anytime."

"Good. I'll bring some over tomorrow."

"I'll tell the boys you're coming. They'll be excited. They keep wanting to know where 'Thumsta' is."

"They're two fine boys, Shelly. You and Bill should be proud. You ever want to sell 'em, let me know."

"That's a definite no sale. I hear you had Fred out on the river."

"I did. I think he enjoyed it."

"I know he did. Maggie said he was like a kid talking about it. She said it was a good thing those fish were already cleaned. Otherwise, they would have been trekked all over the neighborhood and put on display."

"I hear about this Maggie person, but I never see her."

"She takes the early train to Stockford. Gets home after six. Pretty much she's around over the weekends. She mentioned that she'd like to go fishing with you sometime. Oops. Customers coming. See you."

CHAPTER SIXTEEN

JOURNAL - September 3

When I reflect on the freedoms I have lost, the ability to walk, to bathe completely by myself, to cut the meat on my plate, I am led to think of my life in terms of freedom. Every freedom involves an ability, and every lost freedom a lost ability. I have lost many abilities, but I have not lost the possibility of what is the greatest human freedom, the ability to love. Thinking of life as a climb to this freedom helps me track my progress, but also shows me that I am still a voyager. The ability to love is the center of my petition in prayer. It is the focus of my thoughts through each day.

I do what I am able to do for my family and my close friends. It puts no stress on my ability. When it comes to making myself a neighbor to strangers, my ability runs up against some tension, but I still manage. I make an effort. Jesus spoke of the mountaintop goal of love and freedom. "But to you who hear, I say, love your enemies, do good to those who hate you, bless those who curse you, pray for those who mistreat you." (Luke 6:27ff)

When I imagine how free I would have to be to love an enemy, I realize the distance I have yet to climb. There are times when God seems my enemy. Do I need Lou Gehrig's disease? When I think of the treatment given by my peers to Maggie, her enemies become mine. I track my climb by two barometers, my ability to accept others, and my ability to forgive others. Love of others begins with accepting them as equals. There can be no hierarchy or caste in love. I am quite good at accepting humankind, but not always the individual I face. Nor can I honestly accept others by burying them below my memory. It is only when I put faces to them that I can accept them.

Freedom may begin with acceptance, but it stretches toward fullness with forgiveness. They go together just as God's passion for us incorporates forgiveness before we even ask it. There are moments when I am unable to forgive my peers for what they did to Maggie, or for their immoral misogyny. But, I'm learning. I'll get there. In retrospect it seems incomprehensible that the most difficult forgiveness I must muster is to forgive the institutional church, my own fellow bishops. I have read accounts of parents who have forgiven the murderer or rapist of their child. I marvel at their ability to do that. I am not there yet in regard to my peers, even though I realize they are blind, not evil.

When Jesus invited us to take love and its freedom as our goal in life, he was not laying down some extrinsic or unnatural law on us. We know the truth of this law in our hearts. Our heroes have always been those who gave their all for others. Think of how free within themselves are those who have the ability to give their lives.

It is indeed a steep climb to that freedom. I sense a greater distance above than behind me. Could I lay down my life for Maggie? For a stranger? For an enemy? It is obvious that we are not free of a sudden. We win our freedom in the events of each day by doing and, I trust, by suffering. The important thing is that each of us is a freedom to be achieved. The formula is simple: love of neighbor is love of God. The achievment is not simple.

I am preaching to myself here. It is the rare person, I think, who is free of disabilities when it comes to loving others. Certainly, I am not one of them. A first disabil-

ity lies in knowing what is the caring thing to do. Do I do, or do I do nothing? Do I hug or do I spank? I think the answer is, wade in. Do the best I can. Making mistakes is part of life and of loving. Waiting on the sidelines for a surety that will never come is death to freedom.

I'm tired. There are more disabilities to speak of. Another time.

***

Starchy invited himself to lunch today. Felicity had thrown out the lure of a blueberry pie, his expressed favorite, at his last visit and delivered on her promise this noon. She also informed him that next time it would be his turn to cook. Did he want a suggested menu? He took it in good spirit. I suspect she has something on her mind for his next visit, but she won't tell me what it is. It was good to see him. He looked tired, or maybe troubled.

In my study after lunch I brought it up. "You look troubled, Starchy. Is that job worth it?"

"I'll hang in there, Fred. But I am still troubled about Jack Tyrrell taking it upon himself to bypass the laws of the Church and permit a divorced and remarried woman and her husband to receive the sacraments."

"If you must hang somebody for that, Starchy, hang me. I advised him on the matter. I investigated all the facts. Would you like me to go through them with you?

"She was turned down by the Vatican, Fred. You can't override that."

"Why not? The Vatican was wrong."

"What are laws for, Fred? If anyone can take it upon themselves to disregard them, where would we be?"

"Where would we be if those laws don't serve the gospel message?"

"What do you mean?"

"Are laws supposed to serve people, or are people supposed to serve laws? We should talk about that sometime."

"That might be a very short conversation, Fred. I've got to run. Felicity's invited me for Christmas dinner. I'll see you then if not before."

***

Marvin Principle watched the approach of Moira Quinney through a window of his corner office. How she could hold her head high in this small town escaped his comprehension, after being disgraced by that son of hers. She held a position on the bank's board of directors by the strength of her deposits, replacing her husband at his death. Better on the board than Doc was, he thought, generally being in his cups as he was. Doc never seemed to give a damn about how he came across to people. Can't understand a man like that.

It's not fair, he thought, as Moira passed by the window, how her image had been despoiled by her son, John. Concern over his own public image held primacy in the stuffings and preoccupations of Marvin's mind. At the time John's sexual adventures became public, Marvin had sympathetically offered to quietly replace her on the board if she wanted privacy. He had supposed she would leave Plum and find some sort of religious refuge for herself. He couldn't believe her rebuff to the suggestion.

"My son, John, is a good son, and a good man. He will be an asset to society," she had replied. "I'll keep my seat on the board, thank you."

My God, it's as if having a faggot son didn't faze her.

***

Mary Principle and Danni Rouan were excited as they window-shopped the stores and student hangouts along College Street. It was S.O.A.R. time, three days of student orientation, appraisal and registration. Even the acronym had an air of urbanity and independence. The first day had included an orientation for parents. Marvin Principle and Danni's mother had attended and returned to Plum.

The girls had talked with their counselors, and registered for an identical class schedule. They chose to begin with general liberal arts courses, and then decide later on a specific major. Both leaned toward a teaching career and their selected courses would mesh with that direction.

This was their big city now, fifty-eight thousand people grown to seventy-five thousand with the inflow of students, and filled to the sidewalks with limestone and granite monoliths that housed administration, faculty and classrooms. The founders had given little thought to greenspace. Athletic fields were nearly a half mile from the campus center.

In a bookstore they purchased their required texts and headed back toward their dorm. Grange Hall's name was changed to Grunge by experienced dwellers, as "I live in Grunge. Where do you live?" A modern eight story structure, it was anything but grungy. Mary and Danni's room was on the fourth floor. They dumped the books on their small, serviceable desks. Danni climbed to the upper bunk, hers by the toss of a coin, and sat on the edge. Mary sat at her desk.

"You talked to Hanna, didn't you?" Danni asked.

"Yes, I did."

"What'd she say?"

"She said it would probably come out sometime, and did I want it to come to my dad as a surprise. You know, from somebody else."

"But you haven't told him, have you?"

"How do you know that?"

"You said you would tell me. Do you want it to come from somebody else?"

"Of course not. I'm just not ready, that's all."

"It'll never get easier."

"Every time I think about telling him, I picture a look of horror on his face."

"Your dad loves you like crazy."

"And I need that like crazy. I don't know what I'd do, or how I'd feel if I changed that."

"Parents don't stop loving their kids. Look at Moira Quinney and John."

"You might be right. But Marvin Principle isn't Moira Quinney." Mary brushed a wisp of hair from an eye. "I'll tell him, Danni, just don't rush me. Okay?"

"I'm your friend, Mar. I want you to be happy."

"You think I'll be happier if I tell him?"

"Don't you?"

"What if he puts two and two together, about us I mean?"

"He won't do that."

"How can you be sure? He wanted me to go to a private college, you know. I had to talk my head off for him to allow me to come here with you."

"It'll work out, Mar. We've got each other."

"So, let's get this room together and have lunch. We've got four hours before the train to Plum."

"Let's eat under the oak over at the Student Union," Danni suggested, after their desks were cleared and books put on shelves.

"Fine with me," Mary replied.

The Student Union formed a quadrangle whose main feature was a giant oak tree in its center. The girls pulled sandwiches from a Deli dispenser and took an empty table. Danni made a trip to a soda machine and returned with two cokes.

"Is that who I think it is?" Danni asked sotto voce, nodding toward a nearby table.

Mary glanced toward the woman seated there. "You mean the nun from Plum? It sure looks like her. Let's go find out."

"Pardon us, but are you the Sister Maggie who lives in the old Kelly place in Plum," Mary asked.

Maggie, dressed in a white blouse and burgandy jumper, looked up from her book at the two bright faces. "I am indeed. You know me, but I don't know you. Doesn't seem fair."

"I'm Mary Principle. My dad's the banker in Plum."

"I'm Danielle Rouan. My mom is a counselor at the high school there."

"This is a pleasure. Won't you join me?" Maggie asked. "I'd like to get to know you both."

The girls grabbed their sandwiches and cokes and sat at Maggie's table.

"Are you students here?" Maggie asked.

"We're freshman this year, Sister," Danni replied.

"Just call me Maggie, Danielle."

"Everybody calls me Danni."

"Okay, Danni. And you Mary?"

"Mary's good."

"What courses will you be taking?" Maggie asked.

The girls ran down the list. "Are you teaching here?" Mary asked.

"Only one course, Mary, on church history. Mostly I'm doing research and writing."

"That sounds exciting. What are you writing about?" Danni asked.

Twenty minutes later, Maggie excused herself. "Mary and Danni, it's been a pleasure to meet you. I have an office in Thorson Hall. I hope you'll come visit me when you have time. I'd enjoy that. You are impressive young women."

"What did you think of Maggie?" Danni asked Mary on the train back to Plum.

"I really like her. I feel I could talk to her about anything."

"Maybe we could talk to her together."

***

Emily Martin, Sister Felicity and Paul Staunton's wife, Jan, met at Emily's home. Several early frosts had put an end to all blooms in the yard, and the conversation began on an elegiac tone.

"I've never seen anything so beautiful," Felicity said. "It's so sad to see all the flowers gone. I've promised myself that next summer I will get some color into our lawn. It seems so drab after seeing yours."

"The Kelly's always had wonderful flowers," Jan said. "But as they got older, they just couldn't care for them. Since they died, that lawn has been waiting for someone to tend it. Isn't that right, Emily?"

"I should say," Emily replied.

"I've never done flowers," Felicity said. "Except for the potted kind indoors. Emily, maybe you could help me next spring, you know, to design areas, less spectacular than yours to be sure, and to pick out the kinds of flowers?"

"I'd be proud to do that, Felicity," Emily said. She picked up a note pad. "Now, I think we'd better get to the reason why Pastor Grace brought us together."

"Such a good idea," Jan said, her spirited face betraying her enthusiasm. "I'm so glad I got asked for this one."

"Well, we need someone from each church to make sure we don't miss anyone who needs our assistance," Emily responded.

"You two will have to train me on this," Felicity said. "I love babies, but I've not much experience in handling them."

"Don't you worry there, Felicity. It'll come natural like," Jan said.

"Why no one ever thought of this before, I'll never know," Emily said, "a support for women with babies. I wish we had had something like this when I had my brood."

"Me too," Jan added. "I can remember how stressed I'd get sometimes, the constant, twenty-four hour a day care, never a break. We couldn't afford sitters."

"Who could?" Emily said.

"I felt so trapped at times."

"Well, we've got lots of mothers with new babies who must be stressed and feel trapped right here in Plum. Temple Swift doesn't call Plum the Fertile Crescent for nothing."

"We'll need to get the mothers' names. Dumpster, Temple and the pastors can help us with that too," Felicity said.

Emily looked at a note pad. "Our big job will be to line up the volunteers. That shouldn't be too hard. Who wouldn't give an eye tooth to hold a baby?"

"I've got a bunch of learning to do," Felicity said, "but I'm excited."

"I haven't been this excited since I taught third grade," Jan said.

"As soon as we get the mothers' names, we can talk to them about how we can best help." Emily closed her note pad.

"As long as it includes holding babies, I'll do whatever it takes," Jan said.

***

An Indian Summer day, and Dumpster pulled away from the dock, his passenger seated on a swivel seat put back in the bow where Rover had been parked. A woman fishing companion was not new. He had at one time or another taken Doc Robyn, Shelly and Beth individually out on the river to fish. The women could fish as well as a man. What made it feel different?

The toilet thing bothered him a little. "Aren't no facilities out there if you need one fast like," he'd caution each one.

Maggie's response summed up their common answer. "A bush for privacy is good enough, Dumpster. Not to worry."

He studied the back of her head as he drove upriver. A few strands of silver in her dark hair. Still more pepper than salt, he thought. He would later tell her that his primary memory of their first encounter were the piercing, aqua-blue eyes that drilled him on their meeting at the Turnover.

"Fred tells me you're a professional teacher when it comes to fishing. Would you consider taking on another student?" she asked, and held his eyes for the answer.

If the truth be told, there's few things I'd rather be doing, he thought. He turned the boat into a deep narrow bay, idled to a stop and dropped an anchor. "It might be slow fishin' today," he said, "but there's good sized blue gills and crappies in here." He took a can of bait worms up to Maggie. "You okay with worms, Maggie?"

"I can bait my own hook, Dumpster, but thanks." Maggie took the can.

They fished in silence for a while, an eye on their bobbers.

Dumpster pulled in a fourteen-inch crappie. More silence.

"Tell me about Plum," Maggie said. "Fred's told me what you and the pastors are trying to do. How's it going?"

"Okay, but first it's no longer just the pastors and me. It's lots of folks we've already talked to. All of us are checkin' in with each other and our neighbors. You know, checkin' to see if anybody's hurtin' in one way or another. Not bein' nosy, not tryin' to get into what's private to them, but keepin' a keen eye out."

"Are you finding lots of needs?"

"Oh sure. Everybody needs somethin'. But, there's nobody starvin' in Plum. Some folks could eat better. We found one elderly fellow who supplemented his vittles with dog food. We're already meetin' those needs. Some folks are out of work, and Temple Swift's got a group workin' on that. You meet Temple yet?"

Maggie nodded, yes.

"Don't let his folksy ways fool you. He's got as good a head as you'll find anywhere. Anyway, he's helpin' the folks who are out of work to find new jobs."

"I seem to see a lot of elderly in Plum," Maggie said.

"Yup. And we've got lots of people workin' on that. We've got the meals-on-wheels thing goin'. Watch your bobber. You've got a fish."

Maggie reeled in a blue gill.

"That's a keeper," Dumpster said. "You want me to take it off the hook?"

"I've got it. Thanks." She reached the fish into the trolling bucket.

"Big thing about the elderly," Dumpster continued, "is they kind of get trapped in their homes. We lose sight of them and don't know if they're okay or not. So we're fixin' that. We've settin' up a network of calls every day. They'll call each other, and we'll be callin' them. Gets them back into the social mix."

"That is a real need," Maggie said. "What's the biggest need you've found?"

"Well, I think it's got to do with acceptance. We all need to feel we're welcome in the community, that we've each got somethin' to offer."

"How do you convince someone of that?"

"Well, I like to do it by telling folks I need their acceptance. The idea that they're accepted is right in there."

"Do you really believe that we all have something to offer?"

"Sure, even it it's only our need."

"What do you need, Dumpster? Or is that too personal?"

"No. I need acceptance like everybody else. And I need for Becky to come home." Dumpster went on to tell Maggie about Becky.

"I'll pray for that."

"Thanks. Now I've got both you and Fred on that trail. What do you need, Maggie?"

Maggie thought for a moment. "Like you, I need what applies to everyone. Acceptance, Affirmation. In a more specific way, I need to write a piece of church history."

"Good things in history, or bad things?"

"There's really only one kind of history, Dumpster, accurate and authentic history. I'm struggling with that."

"Why are you writing it?"

"I guess because I was there and can report it first hand." There's more to the why of it, she thought. She'd been talking to Fred, trying to sort that out.

CHAPTER SEVENTEEN

JOURNAL - November 19

As I look back on my own journey, I realize how enclosed I was in a culture that pointed to incidentals as true religious experience. Church leaders, I among them, presented a God who demands attention, rather than a God who loves and nourishes. We pointed to particular devotions promoted by one saint or another, to pilgrimages to this or that shrine, to Christ present in the Eucharist as one there to be acclaimed rather than as someone there to nourish our journey.

My fingers are not up to the task of writing the entire list. My point is not that these devotions are necessarily bad. If they support you, if they enable you to better love your neighbor, they are good. If they do not, they are at best irrelevant. And if they become a replacement for caring, they stand in opposition to the true human freedom of the gospel message.

We bishops bear the onus of having misled people. We distracted them from what is central. Perhaps we fooled ourselves, but I think we took ourselves out of the loving process by placing ourselves above the people, a caste to ourselves, modeled on a God who demands attention and servitude. We did it with our laws, and our theologies, and our unacknowledged thirst for power.

I experience now how my journey has made me a near misfit for what is happening here in Plum. It is a painful lesson, to be a beginner, but I am learning how a bishop might be servant to this process.

***

I have just returned from the pastors' luncheon. Because of the snow, Felicity took Rover and me both ways, door to door.

More and more, I am struck by the skill displayed by these pastors. I include Dumpster in that group. One by one they are turning the citizens of this community toward each other. Their real leadership comes not so much from the pulpit, not from public proclamations, but from the private encounters which are hidden from public view and manifest themselves only in this caring spirit that is becoming audible and visible.

Confined as I am, I nonetheless am aware of what is happening. I hear it in people's voices. I see it in their faces. They are building something rare and beautiful, a Camelot without caste.

Sometimes I am speechless before the enormity of it all. Other times I become anxious, fearful at how fragile and delicate it all is. Starchy could unwittingly destroy it in a single step by removing Jack and alienating Catholics from the others. God only knows what threats Grace and Paul face from parishioners who have their own ideas of how things ought to be. Dumpster, I think, is an anchor.

***

Paul Staunton looked around the conference table at the members of the Pilgrim Church Cabinet. Hannah Stuart presided as moderator. The chairpersons of the various church boards: Trustees, Outreach, Deacons, Fellowship and Education were all present, as was the church secretary and several members-at-large. Marvin Principle, chairperson of the Board of Trustees, sat opposite Paul.

Hannah Stuart led the cabinet through its agenda of board reports, discussions and conclusions. She made the last report of the evening. "As chairperson of the ad hoc Open and Affirming church committee, I'm pleased to announce that the committee has reached its conclusion. In the process we have invited homosexuals to discuss their situation with the committee and interested members of the church. We have invited parents of homosexuals to do the same. And we have had several psychologists and psychiatrists speak to us on their understanding of homosexuality. After all these meetings, the committee and interested members of the church who attended the meetings have unanimously endorsed the recommendation that our church join the movement known as Open and Affirming Churches (ONA), and ourselves become an Open and Affirming Church. We are asking for cabinet approval to put this recommendation before all the members for their vote. Any discussion?"

"We don't have that kind of person in Plum," Marvin blurted. "Why bother?"

"We do have them in Plum, Marvin," Hannah replied, "Probably more that we suspect. For fear of derision and even reprisals many stay in the closet, as they call it. I don't think you attended that meeting, Marvin."

Marvin's color increased. "Waste of time. Besides the Bible says it's wrong. Do we invite evildoers to church?"

"Many scholars don't agree with you on what the Bible says," Paul said. "It is not at all clear. And yes, even if something is a sin, we do invite sinners to church. Isn't that what Jesus was all about?"

"Jesus never had kids. Would you want your kids' environment poisoned by people of that ilk?"

"You missed the meeting, Marvin, where Moira Quinney talked to us about having a homosexual son. She described

John as a warm and caring son. And that certainly is how I knew him," Hannah said. "Warm and caring people don't poison the environment."

"They're mixed-up people, Hannah. I don't want my Mary anywhere near them. That's my stand on this."

"Not mixed-up, Marvin. The national associations of psychologists and psychiatrists say otherwise. Our sexuality is not a choice. It's handed to us. Like red hair is handed to someone," Paul said.

"It's dirty, Paul. Dirt is dirt."

"If there's no further discussion, let's put it to a vote," Hannah declared after a lengthy period of silence.

The vote was nine to one in favor of adopting the recommendation.

Marvin Principle was red faced after the vote. "Paul Staunton," he said, "you aren't fit to be a pastor."

***

Mary Principle walked the long hall slowly, then hesitated at Maggie's office door. She fretted with uninvited spectres of rejection as she knocked softly, half wishing for an empty office. The door opened.

"Mary, what a pleasure."

"Hi, Maggie. Am I interrupting your work? I wouldn't..."

"Not at all. Come in, come in. I need a break and seeing you is perfect. Where have you been? It's been weeks since we talked."

To the side of Maggie's desk, two cushioned chairs faced each other, a small glass coffee table separating them. The table held a blue, enameled vase of bright yellow daisies and a small crystal bowl of lemon drops.

"How's school going, Mary?" Maggie asked as they sat down.

"Okay, I guess."

"Are you enjoying it?" Maggie tendered the bowl of lemon drops.

Mary shook her head, no. "I guess." She felt herself being scrutinized.

"Are you all right, Mary?"

"I.. would it be okay...I was wondering if I could talk to you about some personal stuff?"

"You can talk to me about anything you want to talk about. Isn't that what friends are for?"

Mary tuned into Maggie's eyes, probing for the minutest echo of revulsion. "I'm gay. You know, lesbian." No echo. If anything, Maggie's eyes turned softer, warmer.

Maggie reached across and rested her hand briefly on Mary's forearm. "I can see this is important to you. Why do you think that's so?"

"You know, what will people think?"

"Easy. People who really love you, will continue to love you. Those who are homophobic, or into judging others...well, they're really judging themselves, don't you think?"

Mary was silent for a while. "Are...are you like me? Lesbian, I mean?"

"No. I've always felt attracted to men."

"But you're not married."

"No, nuns don't marry. Our bag is celibacy. So, I have no claim to expertise on sexuality or on sexual orientation."

"People don't think it's normal."

"What's normal?"

"Husband, kids, you know."

Looking directly at Mary, Maggie was reflective for a moment. Then: "Let me tell you something about myself, Mary. We'll be mutual confidants. I worked in Rome, Italy, actually in the Vatican, for a number of years. One time, my job took me to Central America to look into why several nuns had been raped and murdered. Shortly after I got there I was myself secretly imprisoned. In that prison I was beaten and raped."

Mary's eyes widened.

"Now, should I feel bad about myself because of that?" Maggie asked.

"No! Somebody did it to you."

"Then I ask you. Did you have a choice in your sexual orientation, or did 'somebody do it to you,' as you put it?"

"It's the way I am."

"And the way you are is wonderful. I have a dear friend who has taught me this: God never makes garbage. You are as good and acceptable in this universe as any star, or any flower, or any other person."

Maggie handed the bowl of lemon drops to Mary.

Mary popped one into her mouth. "Thanks. I...I'd better get to class."

"Don't stay away so long next time," Maggie said, rising. "I think you need a hug."

Mary floated to class, buoyed by the acceptance of both Hannah Stuart and Maggie. Telling dad doesn't seem so threatening now, she thought.

***

Felicity cradled a baby on her ample lap and silently marveled at the tiny fingers that tried to grasp the bottle. Across the room, Emily sat in a cushioned rocker and fed the baby's twin brother.

"It's Christmas come early, Emily," Felicity said. "Aren't these babies perfect, the toes, the fingers, everything?"

"Oh my yes," Emily replied. "This is the best part of helping young mothers. I don't even mind the diapers."

"Did you see the stress on their mother's face when we came?"

"She needed a break, Christmas shopping or not." Emily touched a paper napkin to a dribble of milk on the baby's chin.

"Next Thursday, Jan Staunton and I are going to take care of baby Michael and clean house at the Miller's."

"And I get to care for Clarence, that little boy with Down's Syndrome. He is the sweetest," Emily replied. "My goodness, David's bottle is empty already."

"Sarah's too. A good burp or two and these babies will be asleep in no time." Felicity put a dish towel on her shoulder, turned the child and tapped gently on its back. "Emily, you know that program where seniors call each other every day?"

"Yes, I do."

"Would you be interested?"

"I can take care of myself, Felicity, thank you," Emily said, a slight bristle in her tone.

"Of course you can, but, you know, if one of us falls and can't get up, well, it's a neighborly kind of insurance policy."

"Well, no one needs to call me."

"Would you call others?"

"I could do that."

"Would you call me? Maggie's gone early. She and I share a phone line. Fred has his own. And he couldn't get up the stairs to check if he did call."

"I could do that."

"The sandman has this baby," Felicity said. She stood and carried Sarah to a crib by the wall. "I'm up, Emily. Can I take your baby for you?" There was no reply. Felicity turned and looked at Emily. The left side of Emily's face drooped and her arms had loosened their hold on David.

"Are you all right, Emily?"

No response.

Felicity took David and placed him in his crib. He began to cry. Felicity returned to Emily. "Emily? Emily?"

A few wispy moans came from Emily. Her eyes opened, a look of fright and puzzlement in them.

Felicity hurried to the phone. Who to call? A list of emergency numbers was taped to the wall above the phone. First on the list was Dumpster. She dialed.

Dumpster rushed throught the door less than two minutes after the call. He took a small green cylinder from a black case and had Emily breathing oxygen within seconds. He took her pulse and blood pressure in time to give them to Doc Robyn who arrived with screeching tires. The township's EMTs and ambulance were right behind Robyn.

Robyn, carrying Emily's medical history in her head, did a rapid assessment and administered the clot busting drug TPA. "Don't be frightened, Emily," she soothed. "You've had a stroke, but we're all beside you now. You'll be okay! Do you hear me, Emily?"

Emily slurred a yes and closed her eyes.

Robyn supervised Emily's placement on the gurney to be sure she lay on the affected side of her body. She accompanied Emily in the ambulance on the ride to Lutheran Memorial Hospital in Stockford, and stayed by her side into the night. She saw Emily's eyes gradually change from fright to trust. "You'll be okay, Emily," she repeated. "And we'll have you into therapy already tomorrow. Isn't that good news?"

Dumpster also stayed at the hospital. He retrieved the Village's oxygen cylinder, drove Robyn back to Plum through a softly falling snow, and stopped to report Emily's condition to Felicity.

***

"King me," Dumpster told Jimmy Trumbull. The two men sat opposite, each on a car-hoist bar raised knee high at Jimmy's Garage. Their checkerboard rested on a battered square of pegboard, which itself rested on a stack of four used tires.

"You got it," Jimmy replied, his grease-stained hand laying a black checker atop Dumpster's single on king row. "But you sure as heck ain't got this game. Not yet anyway." He studied the board.

"You don't go to church, do you Jimmy?" Dumpster asked.

"Nope. You?"

"No. I'm a Bible man though. You ever talk abour religion, Jimmy?"

"Nope."

"How come?"

"It's a goldam swamp, that's how come, Dumpster. You talk about that there Okeefeenookee down there in Georgia, or wherever. To my way of thinkin', wading through that swamp would be a romp in a pasture compared to talkin' religion. Gives me the willies just thinkin' about it." Jimmy moved a checker, scratched the stubble on his chin and said, "Your turn."

Dumpster checked out Jimmy's move, pondered a moment, and moved a checker of his own. "Your turn again, Jimmy."

Jimmy checked the board. "Why'd you ask?"

"The pastors Uptop and me been thinkin' about ways to make this town tighter knit, that's all."

"Now, them's good folk, those pastors. Take that Grace. Ain't never been a nicer person what walked this town. So don't get me wrong. I like 'em all, understand, but as far as I can see, ain't none of them churches worth one, single, solitary cow chip. I see folks I know, and I like 'em, don't get me wrong here, but they go into one of them churches every Sunday, and come Monday, I don't see no difference in 'em. Besides, I don't trust nobody what says they got the full and complete poop on anything." Jimmy's hand reached out to the board. "Your move, Dumpster."

"Nothing gives you the willies, Jimmy." Dumpster looked at his smaller, hard muscled, grease-spattered opponent. "I know you better'n that. A guy don't come home from 'Nam with all the medals you brought and tells me talkin' gives him the willies. As long as I've known you, when was it, third grade? you've never let anybody scare you. Your move."

"That may be so, but standin' up to some guy who wants to drain your body of blood like it's a crankcase full of old oil is one thing. Talkin' about somethin' you don't know nothin' about with another guy you think knows even less, now that's a whole different bag a' cow chips." Jimmy's king went whap, whap, whap, whap. In four jumps he cleared the board of Dumpster's remaining checkers. "Get my point, Dumpster? That's what talkin' about religion gets ya. Beat, that's what."

Dumpster grinned a wry smile. "What's the tally now, Jimmy?"

Jimmy walked to the side wall, wiped his hands on his coveralls and pulled a dirty piece of paper from a nail. He licked a pencil point with his tongue, and made a mark on the paper. "I see it you owe me six walleyes this summer against the two mallards I owe you come fall."

"I guess I better get fishing soon, then. You in on this tighter knit thing?"

"If it helps the town, you can bet I'm in, Dumpster. I'm in, that is, as long as I don't gotta go to some church to do it."

CHAPTER EIGHTEEN

JOURNAL - Christmas Eve

Starchy is a man of law. I know where his perspective of church begins. I've been there. He sees the laws as serving the church. Laws make for such good things as orderliness, consistency, a no-wave society. No waves, that is, for the guys at the top if they ignore any turbulence below. Law maintains the status quo in the traditional concept of the church as a perfect society, a society that has prelates on an upper tier. They identify themselves as the church, as in "The church says..." The people below are asked only, in the old cliche, to pray, pay and obey.

I see now that through my entire life a giant figure has dogged my steps, loomed beside me, a co-protagonist to my own story. It was this institutional church. The pastors and people of Plum have altered my thinking. Something is happening here. Plum is in ferment. Time will tell whether we have vinegar or wine. But I'm betting on wine. Church is happening here.

Church is a happening. It happens when people love each other, when they reach to be their best selves by loving. By love, I mean the sometimes tough discipline of being for others for their own sake. It's "do unto others as you would have them do unto you." The only fuzzy thing about love is to know in particular instances what truly is best for one's neighbor. Church is people, all the people who try to let love guide their lives. Church is not institution, not prelates who hand down laws, not a building, not a juridical construct, not rules and laws, not a collection of beliefs, not anything but people who care for each other. Church is not people bound together by utility, by the common interest of stamp or beer can collecting, by some credal ID tag, or by obedience to laws set down by some elite. The bond is caring -- that's all.

I wonder if I will succeed in giving this vision to Starchy. He is coming to spend Christmas afternoon and evening with us. I will try, but I have a deep understanding of the effort it will take for him. I have experienced in myself a lifetime buildup of threads that have tied my own psyche to his vision of church. That church has its own culture, as does this revisited church. And how do we enculturate ourselves, or anyone, into a new culture unless we go, or they come, to live in it?

I have been blessed by aging, by disease and by the people of Plum. They are the forces that have driven me to question everything. They have given me an inner restlessness that seeks relief, a home.

A clear picture of what church ought to be starts with the simple acknowledgment that everyone is acceptable. The only force that can exclude a person from church is that person freely choosing not to love, not to care for others. We cannot be excluded by sin of whatever kind, by mistakes no matter their magnitude, or by anyone's dictate.

So now a new figure dogs my steps, the caring people, and my mind and heart are so much more comfortable.

***

When I was a child, anticipatory excitement always refused sleep to me on Christmas Eve. Now that I'm a senior, I struggle with sleep after an exciting day. It is near midnight and I sit at this computer, the conversations of the day streaming through my memory.

Starchy came early this afternoon and stayed for Christmas dinner. Felicity sent him home this evening with a boxed blueberry pie. I spent the afternoon broadsiding him with my reflections on what church is, and how theologies, laws and leadership ought to be facilitators in the growth of church, not obstacles to the process. I argued that it is immoral to exclude anyone from the table who wants to be there.

Starchy is not a man to take my utterances without challenge. He knows his theology, and the law, and our traditions. He argues from them forcefully.

In the end we had one kernel of agreement, the one I most sought. The church, in its most fundamental structure is people loving God by loving their neighbor.

I then told him what is happening among the people of all faiths here in Plum, the kinds of caring, other-focused activities. "They have even found ways for me to contribute," I told him. "Every Thursday, Felicity takes me to the hospital in Stockford. I visit with the sick. On Tuesday afternoons I visit the patients at the nursing home here in Plum. I'm not very good at it, but I'm improving."

"I'm sure you are," he said, in a distracted attempt to be complimentary.

I admit I had mentally rehearsed my next question. "If worship is this potluck of caring," I asked, "what do bishops bring to the table?" The cold stare I received told me I'd caught him without a ready response.

"We'll talk about that on my next visit," he said. "You're beginning to trouble my stomach, and I intend to enjoy Felicity's feast."

And a feast it was. Maggie, Felicity, Starchy and me.

***

Marvin Principle walked out of church on Christmas morning with barely a nod toward pastor Paul Staunton. There wasn't much he cared for in church these days. He felt a need to be critical of Staunton rise in him at every encounter. Even the message of "good will toward men" sounded a sour note having come from Staunton's sermon. My God, he thought, when is that guy going to get off this lovey-dovey crap? People need a little hellfire and damnation talk once in a while. Staunton could use a little himself. All this "don't judge your neighbor" baloney. How are you supposed to single out the riffraff if you don't judge them?

He took Mary's arm and steered her toward the parking lot. "Let's go get us some breakfast, honey. I could use a tall stack of pancakes and real maple syrup. What about you?"

Mary pulled a muffler tight around her neck. "I'm thinking waffle, Dad, covered with strawberries and real whipped cream."

Near the door of the Turnover, they met Moira Quinney and her two sons, John and Jeremiah.

"Merry Christmas, Marvin. Merry Christmas, Mary," Moira said cheerfully. "Isn't it wonderful, Marvin, to have our children home for Christmas?"

"Merry Christmas, Moira," Marvin replied flatly. "Yes it is nice." He nodded to the two young men. "Jeremiah, John," but felt a crawling in his body at the sight of John. He put a protective arm around Mary. "In you go, young lady." Inside he took a chair at a table with his back to the Quinneys.

That afternoon, Mary walked into Marvin's study and stood directly in front of him.. "Can I bother you, Dad?"

"No bother, honey. What's up?"

"It's something very personal. I don't know how to say it exactly."

"Honey, just say it. I'm your dad. You need me, I'm there. Count on it."

Mary took a deep breath. "Dad, I'm a lesbian."

Marvin stared at her for a moment. "Nonsense, you just haven't met the right guy." He started to turn back to his newspaper.

"No, Dad, that's not..."

Marvin folded the newspaper. "Mary, when you meet the right guy, it'll be firecrackers and skyrockets."

"No, Dad. I've met lots of guys, dated lots of guys. There was nothing."

Marvin pointed a forefinger at her. "Nothing, that's right. When you meet the right guy it won't be nothing. It'll be something!"

Mary stood her ground. "No, Dad. I'm attracted to women."

"You're too young to know that."

"Dad?"

"Let me tell you something, Mary. When I was a young man in college I was on the wrestling team. One time, another guy and I were sort of horsing around, wrestling. I started to get aroused. Well, you can imagine! It worried me sick for a while. Not for long, though. I got me a girl and, well, never mind the details, but I sure got my head straight in a hurry. Hell, at that age a guy can get an erection riding a tractor."

"What I'm telling you, Dad, is the way it is with me."

Marvin looked at his daughter. "You're the spitting image of your mother, you are. Pretty as can be. You're no lesbian, trust me. Tell you what we'll do. Your mother went to see this psychiatrist over in Stockford when she got down on herself. He fixed her up in no time."

"Dad, I don't want you to waste any money."

"Don't you worry about the money, Mary. You got these feelings and you've drawn the wrong conclusion. You're like a balance sheet that just doesn't come out right. Numbers are off somewhere. Well, this guy will check your numbers and get you to balance. You just trust your dad on this. You're not afraid to talk to a psychiatrist are you?"

"If you insist, Daddy, but..."

"No buts. You're your mother's daughter. You're a Principle. You're all woman, Mary. Don't you forget it."

At Danni's home later that evening, Mary explained. "It's like he didn't hear me, Danni. I told him straight out, but he just kept saying it's not so."

"You told him, Mar. That's what counts. And he didn't bite your head off."

"He didn't believe me, though. What will he be like when he finds out it's true. It's like I'm back at square one with him."

"He loves you. Don't worry about it."

***

Emily Martin slept, exhausted from her early morning therapy.

Felicity stopped at the nurses' station and handed a plate of homemade, chocolate fudge to the nurses, both busy with their patients' charts.

"Mmmm," the blonde one, Kathy, murmured.

"Bad nun! Bad nun!" Marge said, smiling as she pulled the plastic wrap from the plate. "Mmmm, good nun! Good nun!' She exclaimed after taking a bite.

"Not to worry about the calories, girls. You are both much too thin. Besides, I removed all the calories. How's Emily today?"

"About the same," Kathy replied. "It's taking so much longer than we ever dreamed. By the way, is Emily awake when you visit her? She sleeps so much."

"Not usually when I arrive. But then she wakes up before I leave. And we chat for a while. Speech is very difficult for her as you know. She gets very tired."

"Well, go right down, Sister. I saw the physical therapist leave ten minutes ago."

"You're sure you prayed away the calories?" Marge asked, already on her second piece of fudge.

"Guaranteed," Felicity said. "Feed without fear, dears. I'll see you later." She walked down the hall, entered Emily's room and took a seat next to the sleeping woman.

Felicity pulled a rosary from her pocket and began moving her fingers over the beads. At each bead she quietly spoke a simple prayer. "Lord, please heal Emily."

Emily slept and dreamt. She felt desperately frustrated in her dream. She was driving along main street and tried to stop at the drugstore. Her foot refused to move to the brake. She pushed and tugged, but the foot was adamant. She woke just as her venerable Plymouth was about to plow into Dumpster's patrol car. She kept her eyes closed, frustration still rumbling within her body.

Emily heard Felicity's voice softly repeating her prayer. A thought struck her with all the suddenness of her stroke. The thought was clear, as clear as the thought she had when she first laid eyes on Henry. She would marry that man! She knew it! And she had. She knew why she got this stroke.

It's those Catholics, she thought. Of course! It's those Catholics! God gave me this stroke because I got cozy with those Catholics. I knew it when I tried to warn Pastor Grace. There's something evil about them, all of them. I knew it! I knew it all the time! God forgive me. I'll never do it again.

She opened her eyes a slit and looked at Felicity, whose gaze was on the rosary. What to do? Should I just up and tell her to get out of here? Emily fretted with the thought. I'm up to it, she told herself. But no. I'd best talk to Pastor Grace first. She's got to get all of us away from those Catholics. Emily closed her eyes and waited.

Finished with her prayers, Felicity stood, left a get well card on the side table, softly patted Emily's shoulder and left the room.

Marge handed her an empty plate when she went by the desk. "Good nun, that was good," she said.

***

Felicity accused me of dejection stemming from cabin fever this morning and decreed that I would accompany her on a drive about the village as she made deliveries for meals-on-wheels. I assented.

Our route took us to Main Street where we turned north. Just past the *Plum Predicate* building I saw this immense ball of snow facing the road. I wasn't sure at first, but the thought of a mammoth centipede head came to mind. I pointed it out to Felicity who immediately made an illegal U-turn and stopped directly in front of it. From that vantage point we could see down the small incline to where the centipede's body wiggled along the bank of Ferocious Creek.

We watched for a moment as Temple Swift and Beth Halkerston's little daughter, Annie, formed legs on one of the worm's many segments. I counted twenty-eight segments. Temple waved, a look of bliss on his face.

Upon our return after the deliveries, Felicity stopped at the mailbox in front of our house and retrieved our mail. She handed it to me before driving into the garage. I separated the mail in my study and found the week's edition of the Predicate was there. I turned to the editorial page and read the following:

"I write this in praise of children, the ones who are, and the ones we once were. We adults, forced into the so called 'real world' by the push of responsibility and suffering, habitually relegate our own child's world into the past. All too often we tie joy and festivity to that same past. We skip from the past and peer at the future looking at our personal visions of what will restore to us the joy and festivity of our childhood. We look from past to future and ignore the present, the only moment where joy and festivity can be found.

"Is the experience of the present moment limited to children, or to those adults who suffer dementia and literally have no past or future? I don't think so. I have been taking instruction over the past six months from Annie Halkerston, age six, whom you all know. By doing 'fun stuff' with me she has succeeded in restoring the present moment to me, and the joy of the present. Joy is the feeling that emanates from love, the love that is caring for oneself and for others in play or in work.

"Many of you have commented that Temple Swift, yours truly, is different these days. Smiles, I am told, have replaced a certain grimness. Now you know why. I heartily recommend that in your search for joy each of you find your present moment. If you need help, ask a child like Annie."

CHAPTER NINETEEN

JOURNAL - Easter Sunday

Dumpster came for dinner today. I must admit, when he comes to talk these bleak March days take on color. I enjoy his company. I think he does mine. We've begun to talk about things spiritual. He seems comfortable doing so and more often than not initiates a topic.

"About sin now," he said today. "Ben Franklin says 'sin is not hurtful because it is forbidden, but it is forbidden because it is hurtful.' How does that idea sit with you?"

"It sits comfortably," I replied. I went on to give Dumpster my thoughts on the subject. "Sin hurts the sinner. It is only an offense against God inasmuch as it is an offense against oneself, God's image."

I could sense Dumpster's interest. His eyes were fixed on me.

"It is a turning in on self and away from others," I said. "It imprisons us in ourselves. If it becomes engrained in us it can seriously impair our ability to be for others. It is the enemy of freedom, a symptom of our inability to love as we ought. It shows that one has chosen not to image a caring and affirming God, not grow as one's best self, not to be a disciple. It also shows our need for God's enabling presence."

"Not much more to say about sin than that," Dumpster allowed.

Maggie then called us to the feast she and Felicity had prepared, and where Dumpster entertained us with his homespun wit and wisdom

As I sat alone here this evening my mind returned to our conversation on sin. I realized there is more to say about it. It has to do with the disabilities we all have that inhibit our caring, our personal demons if you will. I mentioned them before. Personally, I have always been inhibited by an anxiety that kept me on the side-lines of caring. I felt I needed a safe zone between me and others. My interactions with the people here in Plum have helped me recognize this root wound to my freedom, and gradually heal it.

Each of us has, I think, one such wound that we must discover and root out. For some it may be a passion to judge others, or a need to defend one's image, or the stranglehold of envy or power, or a concentration on personal cost, or greed, or comfort, or lust, or just plain laziness. In traditional theology, often ignored, these wounds are called capital sins. And because one of these has a foothold in us, and habitually absorbs our attention and energy, it lies at the root of our inability to be completely for others, to be free.

All my life I have focused my attention on the sins I commit, the action or inaction. I see that now as a mistake. God has forgiven those before I ask. My attention must go to what in me causes those sins.

These wounds we call capital sins are the ones that operate against the building up of community. These are the sins that these discerning pastors in Plum, and Dumpster, are concentrated on. Know thyself, the wise ones say. And that is why. We must diminish the force of whatever enslaves us, but first we must discover it.

***

He even changed diapers! Twice!" Felicity made the announcement at the dinner table where she, Starchy, Fred, Maggie and Jack Tyrrell were gathered.

Starchy, despite his habitual reserve, beamed and puffed his chest noticeably, unable to hide his sense of achievement. "Still, I don't think I'll make a career of it, Felicity," he said.

"I thought I detected a certain odor about you, Starchy," Fred said. "I decided if that's the odor of sanctity, I'll try a different scent."

Maggie and Jack sat listening, enjoying the banter.

Felicity felt a sense of triumph. She had persuaded Starchy to spend one day a week, his day off, "getting into" Plum's activities, "experiencing the culture," as Fred put it.

Starchy had been reluctant and clearly nervous on his arrival that morning. "You'd better be standing by," he told Felicity.

"I don't know how you persuaded him, Felicity," Fred said. "Do you have a secret witch's potion stashed around here somewhere?"

Felicity feigned hurt, lifting a hand to her chest. "Oh, that wounds me here," she said. "If you're calling me a witch, Fred, you'd better hire a taster before your next bowl of soup."

"No, no. Not that. I didn't mean it that way." Fred's penitential pose was equally feigned. "I could scrub the floor as a penance," he added.

Felicity's laughing eyes betrayed her somber tone. "One thing you can do, Fred, is keep a respectful tongue in your mouth."

"Hear, hear," Starchy said.

"Don't hold your breath," Maggie said.

"It would be the death of him," Jack added.

"I will, I will," Fred said.

Felicity presided. Her ample body exuded confidence. "Next week, our accomplished baby sitter here will help Bill Burg insulate Mr. Trotter's attic."

"To Starchy," Fred said, raising his wine glass. Felicity, Maggie and Jack raised their glasses in unison.

***

Marvin Principle started the Cadillac and pushed the accelerator to the floor. The roaring engine fit his mood. "Damn! Damn! Damn!" He let the engine slow and then put the car in gear. "That guy's nothing but a quack. What do quacks know?" he said aloud. "Psychiatrists are all a bunch of quacks. Quack! Quack! Quack! God, I hate those dumb assholes."

Mary sat silently beside her dad. After a long silence she spoke. "I tried to tell you, Daddy. I didn't want you to spend the money, remember?"

"I don't want to talk about it now," Marvin directed. "I need time to think."

The rest of their drive to Plum was silent, Marvin morose and Mary slumped into the cushion.

Marvin dropped Mary off at their home. "I'll be at the bank. Don't make dinner for me. I'll be late," he said dryly.

When he arrived home that evening, the lights were on and Mary confronted him as soon as he entered. "We've got to talk, Daddy. I can't stand being out of touch with you." She was resolute but on the brink of tears.

Marvin's eyes avoided Mary's.

"I'm still your daughter, Daddy. I'm still the same person you lived with all these years. I can't help how I feel, can I?"

"What will people think, for God's sake?"

"I don't care what people think. I care what you think. You still love me don't you, Daddy?"

"Listen, Mary. You keep this between the two of us, you understand?" He turned and walked to his study.

Mary stared at Marvin's back. "Daddy?" she whispered, a little girl's voice. She fled, weeping, to Danni's house.

Back on campus after the weekend in Plum, Mary went to see Maggie.

"Give him time, Mary," Maggie counseled. "Think of all the people who love you. Danni, me, the people of Plum. Your dad has the problem. He hurts you, but he is hurting too. He'll get over it in time. I'll pray for that."

When spring break arrived, Mary went home to Plum. On the very first evening she escaped to Danni's house. "It's like a tomb, Danni. He doesn't talk to me. It's like he's so deep inside himself he can't see outside. He doesn't see me. I don't know how to change that."

***

On the Monday of spring break Mary went to talk to Pastor Paul Staunton. She had overcome all her tentative approaches to possible help.

"Am I evil or something because I feel this way?" she asked. "Should I kill myself because I'm not made the way my dad thinks everybody ought to be?"

Paul heard her out. "Mary, we know that people with same-sex orientation have been with us since the beginning of history. For God's own reason homosexuals are part of our world, just as are heterosexuals. It seems to me that anyone who questions God's design is more than a bit presumptuous."

"What can I do, though?"

"Maybe others have to help you with this. Have you talked to others about this?

"My friend, Danni, Hannah Stuart and Sister Maggie."

"Did any of them talk to your dad?'

"No. I'm sure."

"May I have your permission to talk with your dad about this?"

"Oh sure. Something has to change."

The next morning, Mary told Marvin she was going back to Stockford to work on a term paper. She needed the library there.

Marvin merely nodded.

***

That same afternoon Marvin erupted when Paul Staunton stopped at his bank office to discuss Mary and her concerns. "Leave it alone, Staunton. Who the hell are you to come in here and tell me how to treat my daughter? We wouldn't have homosexuals if people like you didn't find them so damn acceptable. If you mention this to anyone, by God, I'll...I'll. Get out of here."

That evening Marvin called Mary. "Damn it to hell, Mary. I told you not to tell anybody. Can't you keep your mouth shut?"

"I have to talk to somebody. You won't talk to me."

"Then talk to Moira Quinney." Marvin hung up.

Mary took the train to Plum the next Saturday, talked to Moira, and took the next train back to school.

***

Pastor Grace Jensen sat at Emily's bedside and spoke softly to waken her. "Emily? Emily?" She waited while Emily opened her eyes and oriented herself.

"Pastor Grace," she said, "I'm so glad to see you." She rubbed sleep from her eyes with her useable hand. "Remember how I tried to warn you about those Catholics? Just look at what they did to me."

Grace's eyes widened. "What did they do to you, Emily?"

"It's their fault I got this stroke. Nothing like this ever happened to me until I got friendly with that Felicity and that Fred."

Grace looked with warmth at her loyal octogenerian. "No, Emily. Catholics didn't give you your stroke. You're eighty years old, dear, dear Emily. According to Doc Robyn you had your stroke for the very same reason that thousands of others have strokes. The blood supply to your brain was blocked temporarily by a clot. Felicity and Fred had nothing to do with it. They have been praying for you. Felicity comes here almost every day and visits you."

"They just put on that face, Pastor Grace. Underneath, they're devils. Don't matter that I'm eighty. "I'm good to a hundred and twenty. Those devils hexed me somehow when I wasn't looking."

"No, Emily, not devils."

"Yes, they are devils! I know it! It came to me clear as a bell, and I don't doubt it one bit. It's like God was talking to me, telling me to watch out for those devils. So, I'm warning you again about them. You've got to warn our congregation."

"You'll see things differently, Emily, when you're well again," Grace soothed.

"No! I won't! I know I'm right!"

"Emily, you let me worry about devils, would you please?"

"Well, I'm going to warn all my friends."

Grace left Emily after praying with her for recovery. On the way out of the hospital she prayed for Plum's people and tried to assess the damage Emily might do to all their efforts to come closer. Emily had influence, especially among the Lutheran ladies. Still, you wouldn't think anyone would buy into this devil thing.

On her way home she stopped to talk with Jack Tyrrell. Jack lightened her burden by making her laugh. He took off a shoe and sock, and gave proof positive that he didn't have cloven feet. "Let's get together with Felicity and Fred on this," he suggested.

CHAPTER TWENTY

It seems at times that Dumpster and I have been musing on similar subjects at the same time. I don't know if they flow from prior conversations or are the result of chance.

"What's your idea of worship?" he asked this morning. "Ben Franklin says, 'What is serving God? Tis doing good to man.' Seems to me that's what worship is."

I had been thinking along similar lines. The basic character of worship is found in who we are. To the extent that we are loving, giving persons we are true worship. I used to reserve the word worship to liturgical functions like the Mass. Now I realize that when I speak my worship, I can speak no more than what I am, and what I hope and try to increasingly become, God's image.

You are Love, O God, is my prayer of worship. Help me image you is my prayer of petition. I know you, O God, in the experience of my own loving, for when I am for others, or they for me, You are there revealing Yourself, feeding me with the experience of You.

"I agree, Dumpster," I replied. "True worship is caring for others. But let me ask you a question. I know that I ought to be caring, but sometimes I'm just not up to the task. Either I don't know what is the good thing to do, or I'm too pooped to do it. Do you ever experience that?"

"Oh, you bet. Some days I can barely put a smile on my face."

"So, what do you do about that?"

"Well, I might go out on the river and fish, or take a hike down in the park, or read Ben Franklin's autobiography, or read the Bible. Sometimes I just get quiet and pray. I guess, I do whatever strikes my fancy."

"You get nourishment from all of them? You come away refreshed? You're now able to go back to the task of caring?"

"That's about it. Yes."

"Well, I can't go out on the river anytime I feel like it, but when I'm out there with you I too feel energized. I think what we're saying is that we find God out there. Or at least we refresh outselves in the beauty of God's gifts, signs that God is there to nourish us. In the Catholic Church we call those signs sacraments. Some of our sacraments are sort of formal, like taking communion. We find God's presence there. But the idea of sacrament carries out to the river, the trees, the Bible, people whose smiles lift us up, anything that gives us a sense of God's presence and that God is there for us, to nourish us.

"I got a feeling that's the answer to Shelly Burg's question about why there are three churchs Uptop. We just find God and get fed in different ways."

"I think so. Isn't it that we've been conditioned to take our nourishment differently? And our differences aren't that great, I think. Over time we have turned to slightly different diets, that's all. Shelly was right. We worship down here on the streets. Then we take this song of praise we have become Uptop or out on the river, or wherever, express it to God and fuel our tanks again."

"Do you think that's bad, the different kinds of feed, I mean?"

"It seems to work, doesn't it?"

"Yah, I guess it does. But it seems to me that we could all get together in one chow hall, big enough to carry all those different diets."

"I think it'll happen, Dumpster, sometime. When church leaders come, as they surely must, to experience their exclusions as self-serving, and relinquish their turf wars, they too may become sacraments of God's presence, bringing people together like you, and Grace, and Paul, and Jack are doing."

"Like Starchy?"

"Yes, I think, like Starchy."

"In the meantime, we can still worship together, down here where the action is, isn't that right?"

"That's the way I see it."

***

Summer arrived in late May. Fishermen edged up below the river's wing dams or floated the sloughs in search of prey. Many pulled to the piers at Plum and called food orders to the Turnover from a menu board and phone at the end of each pier.

Mary Principle, home for the summer, served these customers, carrying loaded trays from the restaurant to their boats.

Shelly Burg and Maggie looked out at the client traffic from a window table. "I really like that Mary," Maggie said. "How's she doing as a boathop?"

"She's a workhorse," Shelly replied. "I was surprised when she asked for a job, though. Marvin usually didn't want her to work during vacations when she was in high school. I asked her about that. She said she had to get out of the house. Her pal, Danni, works for Beth over at the drug-store."

Maggie looked out as Mary returned to the restaurant with a load of empty trays. "I wish she were happier, Shelly. She wears that constant smile, but it doesn't carry to her eyes."

"I know that you know the reason for that, Maggie," Shelly said. "Mary told me about herself and her trouble with Marvin. She said you knew."

"I feel so helpless," Maggie replied. "All I know to do is pray for them."

"I know that Paul talked to Marvin," Shelly continued. "But Marvin shut him off immediately. Paul talked to Moira and she also tried. Marvin looked to her like he might break down, but couldn't talk about it. Mary tells me she's living in a mausoleum. The only words spoken are the ones she tries. Marvin's started to stay home and let his staff run the bank. He doesn't attend church anymore either. I suspect he imagines everyone knows about Mary, and he experiences it all as a personal disgrace. How do these homophobic emotions ever get so deeply planted?"

"Beats me. That's why I pray. I believe in prayer, that God will find a way to break through Marvin's blindness, if that's what it is." Maggie looked at her watch. "Gotta run. Errands to do. And Dumpster's taking me out for evening fishing. He's parked his boat at the high pier and I'll meet him there at 5:00 p.m. I'm going to get all I can out of summer and this lovely village. I'll see you tomorrow. Felicity's got some volunteer activity going, so I'll bring Fred to lunch. I can't subject him, or myself for that matter, to my cooking. See you."

***

Late that afternoon, Dumpster controlled their float along the edge of the river's channel with short bursts of a trolling motor. They had half filled a stringer with fish pulled from below wing dams and decided to end the day fishing on a float downstream to Plum. They were silent, joining the growing quiet of bird sounds as darkness increased.

As they approached Plum, Maggie sat on the bow, facing away from the village. Dumpster sat in the stern, the tip of his fishing rod resting on the outboard motor. They were practically invisible to anyone looking out from shore, but Plum itself was patched with light, shade, and darkness from the spacing of its street lights. They were perhaps two hundred yards upriver when movement of a human form on the high pier caught Dumpster's attention. The figure stood on the pier's end and bent to its feet. Must be a loose shoe lace, Dumpster thought, and continued to watch. Then, quickly, the figure sat on the pier and slipped into the water. The move set off an alarm in Dumpster. Water's still too cold for swimming.

"Maggie, pull in your line. Be quick," he said. He had his own line in, the motor engaged and was quickly headed for the pier. His eyes swept the faintly-lighted river. No figure had surfaced. He pulled alongside and grabbed the pier. "Tie us up, Maggie, something's wrong here."

"What is it?"

Dumpster leapt onto the pier, a large flashlight in his hand. "Somebody went into the water, and I didn't see 'em come up." He walked the few steps to the end of the pier, his flashlight scanning the nearby water. Maggie joined him.

He took a cell phone from his belt. "Call 911, Maggie. Tell the dispatcher we need a rescue squad here right away. We may have a drowning." While Maggie made the call he kept watch on the water. A boat line caught his attention. Instead of being curled on its hook, it was in the water, running taut. He reached for it, his eyes still scanning the river, and began to pull it toward him. Then he felt the weight of it. One hand wouldn't manage that load. He dropped the light and pulled fast with both hands. The body surfaced next to the pier, the line secured around one ankle. He pulled the ankle up to where he was able to grab it, and hoisted the body onto the pier.

"Good Lord, it's Mary," Maggie gasped.

"Call Doc Robyn, Maggie." Dumpster gave her the number as he checked Mary for breath. None. Pulse? None. She couldn't have been in the water more than five minutes, he thought. And the water's cold. That works in her favor. He checked Mary's airway and began CPR. Fifteen compressions, two ventilations, repeat, repeat, repeat. The Emergency Medical Technicians arrived and took over. For ventilation they used a bag-valve mask hooked to an oxygen tank.

Maggie watched, praying.

After a minute the EMT's checked for pulse. It was there. Weak. Then suddenly a gasp. Mary had breath. Robyn arrived, checked Mary and quickly injected a drug to help her heart. She then rode in the ambulance with her. On the way to Stockford she plied Mary with questions, checking verbally for any brain damage. "How old are you? What's your name? Who's president of our country?" At the hospital she ordered a CT scan as a further check of Mary's brain functioning, and Xrays to see if her lungs held water. She was concerned about possible pneumonia.

Dumpster and Maggie had followed the ambulance in the patrol car. On the way Dumpster had used his cell phone to relay the events and Mary's condition to her father. They joined Robyn who by then had directed that a Patient Safety Aide be with Mary twenty-four hours each day until such time as Mary's psychiatrist deemed it unnecessary. She also suggested an around the clock vigil by people Mary knew and trusted. Maggie made the calls. She, Felicity, Jan and Paul Staunton, Shelly Burg and Moira Quinney would each take four hour shifts.

Marvin Principle arrived at the hospital while Maggie was making the calls. He joined Dumpster and Robyn. "She must have fallen off that pier," he said. "I never did like her taking that job."

"No, Marvin. Mary tried to kill herself," Dumpster replied quietly. "She tied a pier line around her ankle and slipped into the water. Sister Maggie and I were on the river. I saw her go in."

Stunned, Marvin blurted, "My God, like I don't have enough problems! I thought she was nuts. Now, I'm sure. Did she say why?"

"When we find that out, maybe we can help her, Marvin," Dumpster said. "You calm down now. She's alive."

Robyn briefed Marvin on Mary's condition and explained the precautions she had established. "She'll be watched around the clock, Marvin," Robyn said. "You can come as often as you like. Her system has taken a real beating. She may sleep much of the time."

Mary was already asleep on the gurney when she was brought from her tests. Robyn reviewed the test results, checked Mary's vital signs again, and left directions at the nurses' station. Marvin looked at his sleeping daughter and walked away.

Mary awoke as Paul Staunton was relieving Moira. Moira stayed.

"Why, Mary?" Paul asked.

When Mary slept again, Paul turned to Moira. "Marvin is a member of my congregation, Moira, but he has built up an animosity toward me personally. Do you think you could...?"

***

Felicity stopped at the parsonage to pick up Grace. Fred sat in Rover in the rear of the van.

"What's up with Grace?" Fred asked as Grace approached the car.

"Curiosity did what to the cat?" Felicity asked.

"It'll kill you to tell me, is that it?"

"No."

"You're not going to tell me?"

"Yes."

"Yes what?"

"Yes, I'm not going to tell you"

"Well, you're true to form this morning, I must admit," Fred said.

Grace's entry stopped that conversation. As they drove out of Plum Grace turned to Felicity. "Do you think this might be too much for Emily? I mean, if I don't convince her and she gets all hyper."

"What do you mean, too much, Grace?"

"You know, her heart. She did have a stroke."

"I know, but the stroke was caused by a clot in her brain. Her heart's in good shape. It's got years left in it. Besides, I checked with Robyn. She thinks this is a great idea. Wants to know if it works. Evidently, Emily has been relentlessly vexing her about us devils."

"What's this about devils?" Fred asked from the rear.

"Behave back there," Felicity replied.

"What is this? Fred asked, laughing. "Keep Fred in the dark? How about a paper sack over my head?"

"I like that idea," Felicity said. "A grocery bag, maybe."

At the hospital, they all went to check on Mary Principle. Maggie was there and informed them Mary was sleeping. Could they come back later.

Felicity turned to Grace. "You go ahead, Grace. Fred and I will show up in about fifteen minutes. In the meantime I'll bring him up to date."

"You're going to let me in on something?" Fred asked. "Are you all right, Felicity?"

"Hush. Now here's our plan."

Grace left them and proceeded to Emily's room.

Emily woke to the sound of rhythmic prayer. She kept her eyes closed as she had at each of Felicity's visits over the weeks. Her door would close to that devil when she got home, she'd decided. Not here when I'm flat on my back and helpless. She soon realized that something was different. The prayer was the same, but the voice was different. Emily opened her eyes a slit. There was Grace.

"Pastor Grace, I heard you but I thought it was that devil, Felicity."

"How are you today, Emily?"

"I'm just fine, seeing as how it's you, Pastor Grace."

"Emily, can I ask you something?"

"Of course you can."

"You told me that Felicity comes to visit you and sits there praying for you while you keep your eyes closed. Is that right."

"That's right. She says the same prayer you were saying."

"I know that Fred prays for you everyday. He told me so."

"Devils."

"Emily, do devils pray to God?"

"I guess they hate God. Could they pretend?"

"I don't think so, do you?"

Emily look confused.

"I was praying that same beautiful prayer for you that Felicity used. Do you think I would say a devil's prayer?"

"No, I suppose not."

A voice called from the doorway. "Are you ready for the devils?" It was Felicity who was followed into the room by Fred on Rover.

"Hi, Emily," Fred said. "I came to tell you that Felicity really is a devil."

"If I were a devil with the power to make you ill, Fred, you'd be wearing a zit on your nose every day," Felicity replied.

Emily looked bewildered for a long moment. She looked from Grace to Felicity to Fred, and then started to giggle. "Oh my, I'm such a darn old fool. Of course, you're right. Oh, Felicity, can you ever forgive me?"

"Nothing to forgive, Emily dear. Even my mother thought I was the devil sometimes. And I know Fred thinks so too."

"Your mother was right," Fred said.

Felicity ignored Fred. "We are all going to pray you well, whether you like it or not, Emily."

"I like it. Oh, how I like it," said Emily, and began to giggle again.

CHAPTER TWENTY ONE

Driving back to Plum, Marvin's anger had erupted in a monologue. "Goddam it! What'd I do to deserve this? First, a lesbian daughter. Now a suicidal daughter. Shit! Shit! Shit! What the hell is her problem?" At home he picked up a crystal vase from the foyer table and, walking into the living room, flung it at the stone fireplace, sending glittering shards about the carpet. He went to his den and slumped into a chair.

A dark gloom settled into him, and for hours he sat depressed and unable to concentrate. I'd better take something to sleep, he thought. He noticed the Bible on the side table, picked it up and threw it at a bookcase. He walked behind his desk, pulled a bottle of Canadian whiskey from the credenza, and returned to his chair, swigging at the drink. Toward dawn he woke, still in his chair, gulped again from the bottle, and fell back into a befuddled sleep.

***

At ten o'clock that morning, Moira Quinney rang the doorbell at Marvin's house. There was no answer. She rang again and waited, knowing Marvin was at home because his car was still parked at the front curb. She was persistent, and rang again after a minute. Finally, the door opened and he stared blearily out at her. His clothes were crumpled, his face unshaven.

"Moira, I'm not..."

Moira didn't give him a chance to finish. She pushed past him into the room. "Marvin, you clean up. I'll make you some breakfast. We need to talk."

"But. What the hell's going on. I don't..."

"No buts, Marvin. You get moving. I'll find the eggs and other things. You go!"

Marvin turned and walked toward his bedroom. When he showed up in the kitchen twenty minutes later, he had shaved and changed clothes.

Moira was waiting. "You like your eggs over easy, right Marvin? Seems I remember Selma telling me that."

Marvin was silent.

She broke two eggs into a sizzling pan. "You sit down. These will be ready in a shake. I'll pour us each some coffee." Seated two minutes later and watching Marvin's cautious approach to his food, she said, "I want to share with you things I've never told anyone. I want to tell you about my son John."

Marvin put his fork down and started to get up.

"You sit right back down, Marvin. You can at least listen to me."

Marvin sat, looking at his plate.

"I didn't know that John was gay until after that incident with the other boy. He never told me. When I asked him why later, he said that he didn't know how to tell me. He said he didn't have the courage to tell me. He said that he didn't ask to be gay and wouldn't have chosen to be gay, if he'd had a choice."

"Moira, you don't have to..."

"You just shush and listen to me. All I could see was my son in agony, agony over what people would think of him, agony over what I would think of him, agony over what his father would have thought of him. And I was in agony for him. I didn't know how I could help him. I didn't know what to do. All I could see to do was to tell him that he's my son, that I love him, and that I accept him just as he is. I said those things as clearly and forthrightly as I could. I felt so inadequate. And then I found out that was all he needed."

Marvin kept his eyes on his plate. "I don't see how you did it, Moira."

"It was very easy, Marvin, once I accepted the fact that it doesn't make any difference what other people think. It matters what I think, and what I do about it. And I love my son. He is good. He is one of the most kind and loving people I know. He was the first to think of other people's needs. He'd offer to spade Emily Martin's flower patches before she'd ask. He is a giving person. What more can a parent ask for in a child."

Marvin was fighting back tears. "I wanted everything for Mary. I wanted to give her the best of everything."

"I know that Marvin. And you still can. You can give her everything by giving her acceptance. You have an exceptionally wonderful child in Mary. Do you think she chose to be gay?"

"How do you not care what people think, Moira?" Marvin asked.

"Maybe we should give people more credit. Those who are your friends will always be your friends, no matter what. Should we worry about the few who may judge us differently?"

"I don't know, Moira, I just don't know."

"Do you know why Mary tried to kill herself?"

"I don't understand that. In my wildest imagination, I can't think of a reason."

"She did it for you, Marvin. She thought she was helping you. The pain of seeing you retreating from her, and seeing you so unhappy, and the stress of feeling isolated from you was more than she could take."

"How is that doing it for me? That's nonsense."

"No, not nonsense," Moira said. "You are the very heart of Mary's life. When she experienced your pain and withdrawal from her because she's gay, she thought that pain would always burden you. She would rather die than cause you pain. So she chose to unburden you."

Marvin looked up, eyes wide, staring at Moira.

"Think of it, Marvin. Mary loves you so much she'd die for you. She told Paul and me that she wanted it to be over for you. She tied that rope around her ankle so she'd be found. She didn't even want you to worry what might have happened to her."

Marvin continued to stare.

Moira reached out and rested a hand on Marvin's. "Now she needs you," she said.

"What do I say to her?"

"What's in your heart. You tell her that you love her. You say that you need her. You ask if you can begin again. You might even tell her that, like everybody else, you have much to learn."

***

Marvin entered Mary's hospital room. Her eyes were closed so he sat by the bed waiting. Hesitantly he reached out and took her hand in his.

When she opened her eyes, he tried to speak. "Mary, I...I'm a damn fool."

She looked back at him, but didn't speak.

"I...I love you, Mary. You're my life."

Mary reached her other hand over and covered his.

Tears formed in his eyes. "I need you in my life, Mary. I hope we can start over. You know your dad can be a real dunce-head."

"I'll still make you proud of me, Daddy."

"I'm already proud of you, Mary. All I want for you is for you to be happy."

Mary opened her arms and Marvin bent to embrace her.

***

Driving back into Plum, Marvin took the road to Uptop and stopped in front of Paul Staunton's parsonage.

Paul answered the doorbell. "Hello Marvin. Come in."

"No need to come in, Paul. I've just come from seeing Mary. Moira got my head straight on this gay business. You were right, and I've come to apologize."

***

Temple Swift pulled his van into the driveway behind the Predicate building. Tired and relieved that the week's edition was now in the hands of its readers he thought of Mary Principle and his mention of her in the paper. Under a regular weekly heading "Thoughts and Prayers For the Sick and Ailing," he had included Mary "who is in the Stockford Hospital recovering from a river accident." Just the important stuff, he thought, and said a prayer for the girl.

In his office he changed to a muddied pair of trousers and jacket and, whistling, went out the side door to the creek. His afternoon was free and the *project* awaited. As he removed the plastic tarp his mind reviewed the lessons he had received from Annie. Whistling had been one of them.

And he'd taken to it. Snappy, happy tunes only, Annie instructed. No sad stuff. For the last few days he'd been whistling "Dixie," literally. Due for a change one of these days, he thought. Wish I could sing as well as I whistle.

During the tail end of the past summer and into early autumn he and his godchild had caught frogs and butterflies, and built an honest-to-goodness tree house in a huge cottonwood near the creek. It was not large enough for Temple's bulk, but accommodated Annie and one or two of her own age friends. Temple would sit outside on a limb and receive instructions on his next lesson. He cleared a brushy area for Annie and her friends to put on plays written by them for their customers. One dime per ticket. They always had a part for him to play, as a tree, or a house, or a horse.

He and Annie had marched the creek like pied pipers, blowing on imaginary flutes made from twigs. And they had engaged in and sponsored mud pie contests. He recalled some of the more creative pies, decorated with flowers, asters and daisies, and with little stones for jimmies.

The pies had led to this project. Annie decreed they would build a mud castle of bricks, dried like the pies, in the sun. When the finished castle, complete with courtyard and crennelated ramparts, covered a rectangle about the size of Temple's desk, Annie declared it to be too small. She then stepped off an area, roughly nine square yards. "We want it that big," she said, her face flushed with contentment.

They had filled the space, extending the castle, adding courtyards, ells, and lesser buildings, each with a purpose. At the end they encircled the entire area with a foot-high wall topped with a battlement. Eventually the project began to draw villagers, many of whom found ways to contribute. Jimmy Trumbull brought a sack of ball bearings to make pyramids of cannon balls next to the cannons on the wall.

Temple ensured that a tarp covered the entire structure when not under construction to prevent rain or snow from reducing it to globs of mud. Now he picked up a spade and began the final task. A moat. He would channel water from the creek to circle the castle walls, and then return to the creek. He had just taken the last spadeful and watched water fill the moat when Annie appeared.

"Wow, Mr. Swift. That's the bestest. Isn't it the bestest ever?" she asked. She got down on her knees and dipped her hand in the flow.

"Yes, Annie. It is the best mud castle ever made. I'm sure."

Annie wiped her wet hands on her jeans and dug a crumpled paper circle from her pocket. On the circle, in uneven letters, she had printed: DIPLOMA IN FUN STUFF. She handed it to Temple. "You're really fun, Mr. Swift. Mom gave me the words for the deeploma. She said I should give you a hug with it."

"Thank you Annie. I feel like I'm fun, thanks to you. And I'd really like a hug." Hoisting her up, he felt her arms tighten around his neck. "You're a good hugger, Annie, like you're a good teacher." The tears that began to well up in his eyes came, he knew, not from sadness, but from a rediscovered fountainhead of joy.

He put Annie back down and they stared for a while at their completed castle.

"Let's go celebrate with a double-decker," he said.

CHAPTER TWENTY TWO

JOURNAL - August 8

I am slowly gaining skill at operating this computer with my eye movements. The words appear slowly on the screen, but now with accuracy.

This noon I drove Rover to the Turnover. I eat at home with Felicity's assistance as I can no longer raise my arms. But I can drive Rover with a mouth-operated joy stick, a freedom I relish on warm August days like today.

Our group of pastors was meeting and I couldn't bring myself to miss the news. They talked about the village. Plum is so well knit, they felt, that it calls for a celebration.

Grace suggested a festival. Everyone concurred. I recalled a line from the philosopher Josef Pieper. "A festival is a phenomenon of wealth; not the wealth of money, but of existential richness." And St. John Chrysostom said, "Where love rejoices, there is festivity." That's what we have in Plum. A richness in our living that springs from a caring that is joy, a joy that wants an expression. Why not a festival?"

***

Starchy McIntyre felt the soreness in his arms and legs as he walked into Fred's study in the late afternoon of August's last Friday. "I'm beat, Fred," he said. "I've been on a clean-up crew all day out in the park. Lord, I hurt all over."

"Take a load off those legs, Starchy. You need a rest, and so do I. This thinking all the time gets wearisome. Look at this." He pointed to a radio like gadget on his desk. "A button to communicate with the whole house, and a button for every individual room. Watch this." He bent his head slightly and poked a stick at a button with his mouth. "Fred to Felicity, Fred to Felicity," he spoke at the machine. "Are you there, Felicity?"

"Nobody's here," came a response.

"Nobody's good enough, if Felicity's out. Better maybe."

"Nobody likes a smart-ass," came the voice. Smart-ass types don't get fed."

"I'll flog myself in contrition. Meanwhile it's time for you and Maggie to join Starchy and me for the children's hour."

"Is Starchy there?"

"I'm here, Felicity."

"Well, that's different. We'll be there shortly. Maggie's pouring the wine as I speak. A dollop of arsenic in Fred's, Maggie. Signing off."

"Conversation is the only exercise I get these days, Starchy. I don't know who's the toughest trainer, Felicity or Maggie. Life is so wonderful."

"What's so wonderful about it?" Starchy asked softly, looking at Fred's wasted frame and wincing inside. "What's so wonderful about life with ALS?"

Fred smiled. "You are here for the weekend, my friend. Felicity and Maggie are here. And I'm about to enjoy a glass of merlot. That's wonderful. And it's enough."

Starchy began to choke up at Fred's words. It went unnoticed when Maggie entered carrying a tray. Felicity followed with hor's d'oeuvres. Setting the tray down, Felicity gave Starchy a hug, then put a bowl of nuts and one of raw vegetables on a coffee table. She carried a glass filled with a chocolate colored concoction to Fred. "You'll never guess," she said as she set it down and put a long straw in the glass. "No dinner for you until this is all gone."

"Tyrant." Fred pulled the straw from his wine glass with his lips and waggled it. "Cheers," he mumbled through the straw, and then pushed it back into his glass. "I think Starchy is about to flay Felicity for signing him onto that cleanup detail today. How about that for great entertainment! What's she done to your tomorrow, Starchy?"

"Roustabout duty. I get to help pitch that huge circus tent in the morning. In the afternoon I'll meet with the pastors on the prayer service."

"Starchy, you've been involved in Plum for over six months now," Maggie said. "Has it been worth it?"

"I'm a changed man, Maggie. I am in your debt, the three of you and the people of Plum for removing the stained-glass spectacles I used to wear, and helping me experience the world as it is." Starchy took a sip of wine and continued. "Fred, you've been bludgeoning my brain about how we bishops have made ourselves a caste above the rest of mankind and taken on the lifestyle of the aristocracy in the Middle Ages. Well, I've here to tell you that you were in error on one major point. Sure, we've got the trappings, the insignia, the thrones and royal robes, the gold and jewels, the wealth or at least access to it, indolence if we choose it, and we don't answer to anyone except higher titles in the clerical pecking order." He paused.

"So, where was I wrong?" Fred asked.

"We are not like them in one significant detail." Starchy removed his glasses, tilted his head back and looked down his nose. "It is reliably reported that *they* all smelled like skunks."

Felicity's last sip of wine spurted out in a fine mist. She was alternately laughing and choking.

"Are you all right, Felicity?" Starchy asked.

She nodded.

"I am indebted to you especially, Felicity. If you had not engaged me with others in the works of caring here, it would all still be an intellectual exercise for me, an abstract involvement from the remoteness of my castle. From which distance I would enforce laws that sound lovely, but serve mostly to control, I would dangle honors that are meaningless and propose devotional substitutes for caring. I would dole out from above without ever engaging in the face to face action of caring."

"And you were right, Fred. Fooling ourselves that we were enslaving others to Christ, we bishops have only enslaved ourselves. We have created a prison for ourselves with the privileges that keep us in, and rules that keep others out. If I'm right, our problem is simple enough. We bishops are unable to trust, that indispensable component of love. We are unable to put our prestige and esteem in the hands of others and let others judge us on our merits, as every other human must. We attempt to secure esteem with power and the insignia of power. And we never get the real thing. We may land a bit of deference, but never love or respect. We are addicted, consciously or unconsciously, to power, and that addiction takes us away from love. I think we need to have it taken from us."

Felicity and Maggie began to applaud, clapping quietly.

Starchy moistened his mouth with wine. "Here in Plum, I have experienced the wisdom out there in the people, wisdom about daily life, about how to care. The presence of God's Spirit is palpable in them. But do we bishops listen? Do we carry their Spirit-wisdom upwards to the Vatican? It hasn't happened since the time of Paul and Peter. We only carry things downward: rules, morality conceived in the remoteness of clerical caves, everything but love."

"Hear, hear," Maggie said.

"It's true," Felicity added.

"Don't you think bishops must turn to reality?" Fred's question was rhetorical. He continued. "Look at the leadership given here by Grace, and Paul, and Jack, and Dumpster. Leadership in caring. We were discussing Sunday's liturgy the other day and got stuck, briefly, on the Communion part. Our rules say one must be Catholic and worthy. Jesus never asked anyone if they were worthy of His presence. Nor did he demand any kind of dogmatic understanding of Himself. God is present to all, saint and sinner. Who are we to change that? Are we protecting God from the unworthy? And who are we to say who is worthy?"

"You're right," Starchy said. "We don't have time to change all the stupid rules. The only answer is to ignore them."

"Even if it's your butt in the wringer?" Fred asked.

"If anyone's butt goes into the wringer, mine should be first. Otherwise, how can I call myself a leader, a pastor?" He began to chuckle. "Six months ago, if I found out that Jack thought like that, it would have been his butt, and I'd have been the guy running the wringer. What have you guys done to me?" He raised his glass. "Whatever it is, thanks."

Felicity stood. "Dinner is served in five minutes," she said. "Don't say anything important while Maggie and I get it on the table."

***

Light flowing through her window woke Maggie in the late hours of the night. She looked out and discovered its source to be light from Fred's window below, reflecting from a blue spruce tree. Concerned, she threw on a robe and went downstairs and into his study. She knocked and opened his bedroom door a crack. "Are you all right, Fred?" she asked.

"Yes, I'm okay," he replied. "You may come in, Maggie. I'm decent."

Maggie pushed the door open, lifted some books from the chair next to his bed, and sat. "It's two o'clock in the morning, Fred. You need rest. Tomorrow, I mean today, will be a strenuous day for you. What's keeping you awake?"

"Just thoughts, Maggie. I've been thinking of Starchy, of my homily, lots of things."

"What is it about those things that can't wait until morning?"

"Nothing really. But thoughts are life to me now. Take Starchy for example. I mean, the change in him. I am struck with wonder at how, when we accept others who think differently from us, they can then truly hear us, and we them. It only increases my conviction that God's Spirit is alive and at work in the world, and here in Plum. The Spirit was with Starchy, turning his understanding so that goodness could find a way out, and love in. The Spirit was with you and Dumpster when you were in the right place on the river to save that wonderful young lady from her despairing action. And the Spirit was with Grace and Felicity when they turned Emily's opinion of Catholics away from devils."

"Grace is everywhere, isn't it?"

"Yes. Grace, God loving us, is the one constant in our universe. You are Grace to me, as is Felicity and the caring people of this village."

"And you to all of us. I doubt if you realize the power of your example." Maggie reached for Fred's hand. "I pray every day that you will be with us for a long, long time. God is in for a taste of Irish anger if that's not the case."

"Maggie, when I take my daily inventory, I try to count the muscles that still have some function. It's a short list."

"Are you strong enough for your homily today? Someone could read it for you."

"No, I need to deliver this one myself. And I know I can do it. For one thing, it's short."

He chuckled. "For another, Felicity has given me the confidence. She told me that my tongue will be the last muscle to go." He paused and looked at Maggie. "God bless her for her gentle badgering, and for laughter."

"She loves you too, you know. She badgers both of us, but she'd die for us."

"And I for her, and for you."

Maggie pulled the bed covers closer around Fred's neck and tenderly touched his cheek. "You sleep now." She reached and turned out the light using the remote on Fred's wrist.

***

A morning sprinkle had given way to deep blue skies. The temperature hovered near eighty degrees. It was noon on Sunday, August 28th, and the parking lots of the three churches Uptop were filled, the people waiting in their cars. Dumpster turned on the flashing lights of his patrol car and led. Car by car the lots emptied as the cars followed him down the long gradual drive. At Main Street, the parade turned south, picking up more cars from the parking lots along the way. The line of cars drove past empty sidewalks and out of the village, stretching from the village limits to the park where Dumpster turned in. At the entrance students handed activity schedules to anyone who had missed the one printed in the *Predicate.*

Along the circle drive of the park, cars pulled into the lots of their choice, some at the ball fields, some at the children's playground with its swings and other equipment, some at the park's docks where boats had been parked, three astride, by their owners. Games began at one o'clock. The soccer competition was girls vs. boys. Softball was seniors vs. juniors, the dividing line set at age fifty. A fishing contest, open to two-person teams, would award first prize to the team with the weightiest catch of legal fish. A cooking contest would be judged by Emily, Felicity and Jan Staunton on the desserts brought for the evening meal. First place in a playground contest, open to all ages, would go to the one who pumped highest on a swing without assistance. A three-legged sack race was open to all ages.

Five hundred plus people quickly divided into contestants and spectators. At three-thirty o'clock a student turned on Dumpster's siren for a thirty second blast to signal the end of all games. The girls had won the soccer game thanks to the skill and speed of Mary Principle and Danni Rouan. Dumpster and Maggie, with a mess of striped bass, lost out by two pounds to the teenage Johnson twins, who came in with three giant catfish. The seniors won the softball contest thanks to the fast pitching of Jimmy Trumbull. Doc Robyn won the cooking contest. Temple Swift came in a respectable fifth in the swing contest, losing to Annie and three other grade schoolers. Moira Quinney and Marvin Principle placed third in the three-legged sack race. Jack Tyrrell and Paul Staunton came in second behind a pair of high school runners.

At four o'clock the entire throng gathered on a fresh cut meadow and took seats at round tables, ten to a table. Men quickly carried from the tent segments of a stage, the tent unneeded on this sunny day for shelter. They reconnected a microphone and speakers on the stage. A lectern was placed on the left side of the stage, a table in the middle front. Bill Burg and a helper affixed a wooden ramp to the back of the stage.

Fred drove Rover up the ramp and moved next to seats occupied by Grace, Paul, Jack and Starchy. Temple Swift moved to the lectern and quieted the exuberant crowd before a string ensemble of local seniors played a medley of Vivaldi, Bach and Mozart. Then, accompanied by the ensemble, Temple, in a somewhat quavering voice, led the crowd in singing "America the Beautiful."

Grace replaced Swift at the lectern and read an opening prayer:

"Love to you and peace from the God of us all. Let us pray.

Dear God

You love us beyond our ability to understand. Increase our understanding of this love.And let this understanding go to our minds, and to our hearts, and then our hands, and through us to each other. In your Holy Name. Amen."

The crowd thundered their Amen.

Mary Principle rose from a nearby table and stepped onto the stage. At the lectern she read from St. Paul's letter to the Galatians:

"God has called you to freedom. Do not lose your freedom by turning in on yourself; rather, serve one another through love. For the whole law is fulfilled in a single statement, namely, 'You shall love your neighbor as your-self.'"

With the accompaniment of the ensemble, Temple chanted the variations of Psalm 118 on the enduring love of God for us.

Dumpster came to the stage to read the gospel story of the good Samaritan, the unclean man who, unlike the man's own countrymen, made himself a neighbor to a man wounded by robbers.

When Dumpster finished, Fred drove Rover to the side of the lectern and waited while Dumpster came and adjusted the microphone.

"My friends,

"In my many years of trying to be a servant of God's design, I have never before delivered a homily about myself. I am at least a part of this homily because it is about us.

"When I arrived in Plum a little more than a year ago, I was a drifter, adrift for the first time in my life from the conviction that I knew God's design, adrift too and anxious within my own person. I was a man looking for peace in my beliefs and in myself.

"You made a home for me among you. The joy of caring that radiates from each of you made me comfortable within myself. I know now that a single heart doesn't make a home. Hearts make a home, hearts aimed at one another.

"God's design is simple. Love one another. Be at home with one another. You have made me remember this, and you have taught me the how of it all.

"You have made yourselves neighbors to me in every caring way possible. By doing so you have transfigured my convictions of God's design for us, and brought me the inner tranquility of being at home.

"You are my saints. Thank you. May you ever be aware of God's pleasure in you. Amen."

"Amen" roared the crowd as they broke into applause. Dumpster attended to the microphone and Fred edged Rover back to his spot.

Grace and Paul moved to the lectern.

Paul began. "We know that God is present here with us. We have God's own assurance of that. God is here with affirming love, with acceptance of our faults, and with the forgiveness that wipes away sin before we ask for it."

Grace continued. "Some of us use the word 'sacrament' to speak of things that are signs of this presence of God. A long venerated form of sacrament is the meal, a place where people come together and share. On this table before me are baskets of bread, and goblets of wine. We ask you all to join us in a short prayer and then in the words that Jesus used at his final supper with His disciples. You will find them on the back of your activity program. We will celebrate this sacrament in the context of our own supper. The ladies will begin."

Women: We praise you, O God, for calling our Village to this Day of Freedom, the freedom of caring.

Men: We rejoice, O God, and praise You for making us conscious of our human equality.

Women: We honor you, O God, for all of our differences which, with your aid, we have joined into a single, caring community.

Men: We remember how Jesus drew his friends together for a final meal on the evening before he died.

Paul held up a basket of bread.

All: Jesus took the bread, broke it, and said: Take this and eat it. This is my body given up for you. Do this in memory of me.

Women: Then he took up the cup.

Grace held up a goblet of wine.

All: He gave You thanks, O God, blessed the cup and gave it to his friends with the words: Take this, all of you, and drink it. This is the cup of my blood, which shall be shed for you and for all for the forgiveness of sin. Do this in memory of me.

Two people from each table came forward and returned to their table with a basket of bread and a goblet of wine, passed them around, and returned them empty to the stage. On the stage, Jack Tyrrell passed the basket of bread, followed by Starchy with the goblet.

The stage emptied and table by table the people filed along on both sides of a catered food line.

"You guys ought to practice your soccer more." Mary Principle needled John and Jeremiah Quinney at the table they shared with Moira, Marvin, Danni and her parents, and Jan and Paul Staunton.

The two young men wore sheepish grins. "We'll be ready next year," John said.

"Now if this is what religion is all about, I could cotton to it," Jimmy Trumbull announced to Starchy, Dumpster, and the rest of the people at his table.

After the meal, people roamed about from table to table. Dumpster stood, observing from the edge of the assembly. Must be ninety per cent of Plum here, he thought. That's pretty good. He waved at the wheelchair-bound residents from the nursing home. He felt good inside.

The evening ended with fireworks over the river. Beth Halkerston, Doc Robyn and their families, with Temple Swift watched from the bank. Annie sat astride Temple's shoulders. "Ooooh, Aaaah," they jointly exclaimed at each burst of floating colors. And their laughter resounded with the display.

EPILOGUE

Felicity and I attended Mass this morning. Jack and Starchy co-presided. We celebrated Fred's life and his legacy to each of us. Fred died a year ago today.

As I watched Fred dwindle physically over these past years, our friendship deepened. I miss him greatly. When he died, Felicity and I cried for days. Fred and I were friends in Rome. In Plum we became confidants. I came to spend more hours with him, and each day I saw and felt the fire of love's freedom grow in him, in visible contradiction to the horrible wasting process that carried him gram by muscular gram to a final shallow breath.

Until that last breath, acceptance and affirming love, etched in his eyes, greeted every visitor. The memory of his eyes will be for my remaining days both replica and vehicle of God's love, and the power of that love to change us. Fred changed me. God changed me through Fred.

When I knew Fred in Rome we both looked out at our church and saw a need for change we believed could only be achieved through a redistribution of power. We saw the sharing of power as essential for justice and equality. Here in Plum, Fred came to see the deficiency in that thinking, and has led me to a new understanding. To love and rise to the fullness of love's freedom one must eschew any power that is not a gift in love. There exists a radical incompatibility between love and power unless that power is the gift of trust in love. Power outside of that context establishes inequality. Love can only exist between equals.

For the laity, women especially, to knock on the bastioned door of clericalism and request a share of clerical power is as short-sighted as it is futile. We should not desire to exercise power in the way our prelates do, for that power, like all overlording power, corrupts by eroding sight. It causes a blindness securely protected by the fortress walls of *good intentions* and the moat of *pious rationalizations.* Power among our prelates tries to present itself as competency while it dilutes love down to the tepid broth of a dole. Dole, a matter of justice, does not rise to the status of love. That power knows nothing about love as freedom. Fred has enabled me to see that power, as Christ envisioned it, is embedded in the trust given by one person to another. That trust alone grants authority. When the trust goes, so goes the authority. The Freds and Starchys who break loose from clerical power's addictive hold do so only by meeting the eyes of every other human as an equal. Such bishops are few, and are generally shunned by their peers.

It is a gross understatement to say that I was angry when male clerics shut down the Vatican Department of Justice. I felt as if the entire history of clerical suppression of women fell on me personally. I was in a rage. My guts were on fire. I realize now that revenge fueled my writing of the department's birth, history and demise. I wanted the despoilers exposed and shamed. Fred was the surgeon who drained the anger from my veins. And the people of this village were his assisting phlebotomists. Anger is wonderful. It can motivate, but it can also be self-destructive. Love motivates, but is never self-destructive.

The history of the short-lived Vatican Department of Justice has been published and sits, collecting dust, on college and university library shelves. There it is available to the stray scholar to provide a footnote to their various investigations. The male hierarchical structure continues to trumpet patriarchy as if it flows from God and not from their self-interest.

Next week we will celebrate the fourth annual Plum Festival Day. You may be interested to learn where the people of this brief history are now in their lives.

Mary and Danni graduated this spring and have already secured teaching positions. They have an apartment in Chicago and are in the process of adopting a baby boy. Marvin's eagerness for that grandchild outsizes that of any child's for Christmas to come. Marvin and Moira Quinney, to no one's surprise, married at the second Plum Festival Day. Mary served as bridesmaid, and Moira's son, John, as best man. John, after working several years at a San Francisco financial institution, is now running the Plum bank, with Marvin providing less and less oversight. Moira and Marvin are often away on tours of one kind or another. But I'm sure that baby will keep them more at home.

Grace and Paul are still in the harness, though Grace has announced her retirement at the end of this year. She and Dick will continue to live in Plum, but she fully intends to do so in the manner of Oscar Petersen, her non-interfering predecessor who passed away two years ago. I've seen tears in her eyes when she is asked whether they will move to a kinder climate. "How could I ever leave this wonderful, free people?" she replies. The rest of us know how much she has contributed to our freedom.

Paul says he is still having too much fun to retire. Jan tries to hold him back for his own sake, but fails. Then again, Jan is herself a whirlwind, another Felicity when it comes to activity. They are both happy and on the go. I have often witnessed the respect the villagers hold for Paul when they meet him on the street. It shines in their demeanor.

Dumpster regularly takes his lunch at the Turnover. Becky is a waitress there for breakfast and lunch five days a week. I was privileged to witness the reunion of Becky and Dumpster last summer. Dumpster and I had been fishing one evening. There was a figure standing on the dock when we returned, not identifiable in the growing darkness. Dumpster jumped to the dock to lend me a hand.

The figure approached just as I stepped onto the deck.

"I'm home, Dumpster," she said.

Dumpster turned to her, speechless for a time. "Becky."

"I'm home to stay if you want me to," Becky repeated. "It's a big world out there, but it's not real adventure like I thought. Places are like stuff. They don't give back to you. They only give a short thrill and then the adventure is gone. I was wrong. Adventure is in people. And you're the adventure that I need and want."

Dumpster wrapped his huge arms around her. "Welcome home, Becky," he whispered. "You're all I need to fill all the empty space inside me." His face, over her shoulder, was turned toward me and I saw the tears fill his eyes. "Prayers *are* answered," he said aloud. "I always knew they would be."

By chance and good luck I was alone with Fred at his final moment. The muscles of his face could no longer produce the smile that was reflected by his eyes. His journal reveals the belief perspectives that brought him contentment. His eyes revealed his inner tranquility.

I tried to thank him for his gifts to me, the same gifts that gave him peace. I held his hand and said simply, "Thank you for you, for your friendship."

He looked at me with eyes full of affection and gave me another gift, his last words, uttered haltingly with obvious difficulty: "Never be afraid to die, Maggie."

Dear Reader,

Wind-borne Publications is a very small press. Our marketing is limited to the good word passed around by our readers. If you think that this story and its theme are worth circulation, please pass the word. We appreciate it. *Wind-borne.*

Order Form

____copies of *Unless A Grain of Wheat*
____copies of *Dead Men's Bones*
____copies of *Called To Freedom*

Name:____________________________________

Address:__________________________________

City:____________________State:____Zip:__________

Phone:(_____)________________________________

Direct Mail Price:
$10.00 per copy # copies____ $__________

Postage and Handling:
$2.00 per book $__________
Total: $__________

Please make check payable to Wind-borne Publications.
Send order and check to:

Wind-borne Publications
P.O. Box 733
Hales Corners, WI 53130